ATTACK ON AREA 51

ATTACK ON AREA 51

Mack Maloney

OPEN ROAD

INTEGRATED MEDIA

NEW YORK

Copyright © 2013 by Mack Maloney

Cover design by Michel Vrana

ISBN 978-1-4804-4419-5

Published in 2013 by Open Road Integrated Media, Inc.
345 Hudson Street
New York, NY 10014
www.openroadmedia.com

ATTACK ON AREA 51

PART ONE

NIGHT OF THE TWELVE BOMBERS

CHAPTER 1

THE UFO APPEARED AT MIDNIGHT.

Two radar techs attached to Football City's Air Force were the first to spot it. Sitting on a hill twenty miles north of Football City, their dilapidated little hut had only one working instrument: an ancient air defense radar that could detect objects up to one hundred miles away. At the stroke of twelve, it lit up like a Christmas tree.

It had been a sleepy, damp night up until then. A thunderstorm had been raging outside for hours; rain was leaking through the hut's tin roof, keeping both men on bucket duty. The hut was one of only a handful of sites that provided Football City's early warning system, and it was a small miracle that the radar was working at all. Most of the city's military equipment was so old it was practically useless.

"What the hell *is* that?" one tech exclaimed on first seeing the strange blip.

"It's way up there," the other replied, adjusting his screen for a better view. "But it's coming down damn fast . . . "

The object was entering the atmosphere from outer space—something that was theoretically impossible. Like the rest of the world, the American continent had become so fragmented in the past decade that just getting a few ordinary aircraft in the air at the same time was a major accomplishment. Nothing had been shot into space in more than ten years; no one had the capability to do so. The only things seen falling from the sky these days were meteorites and old space junk.

But the techs knew that was not the case here. Not only did this large object appear to be under intelligent control, but it was steering its way right toward them. Used to looking for low-flying enemy aircraft belonging to Football City's host of hostile neighbors, they'd never seen anything like this.

"We better call HQ," the first tech suggested, sleepy no more.

The second man had already grabbed the phone.

"You don't have to tell me twice," he said.

Ten miles to the south, an old Huey helicopter was battling its way through the same thunderstorm when its radio burst to life.

The call was from Football City's military headquarters.

Too busy wrestling with their controls, the two copter pilots ignored the radio at first. They'd been on a routine patrol of Football City's outer defenses when the storm hit. Before the Big War, people in America knew what kind of weather was coming two weeks ahead of time. These days, violent storms always came as a surprise.

Both men were actually fighter pilots; normally, they wouldn't be caught dead flying an eggbeater. But because Football City's military was in such a degraded state, fighter planes were extremely hard to come by. That's why these two fighter jocks, JT Toomey and Ben Wa, found themselves flying copters.

Finally JT pushed the RADIO RECEIVE button. The signal was weak, but he caught enough of the message to understand how strange it was.

A huge, unidentified flying object was falling out of the sky and heading for Football City. The copter pilots could probably see it if they simply looked up.

Both pilots laughed. There was so much rain and lightning

going on around them, they thought it would be impossible to see anything else.

But they were wrong.

Looking out the glass roof of the copter, they were astonished to see a gigantic ball of flame coming right at them.

"*What the fuck?*" Ben gasped, violently yanking the controls to the right to avoid a collision. The fireball roared by them an instant later.

A few seconds after that, the entire eastern horizon lit up like daytime.

"Christ!" JT exclaimed. "Was that a nuke?"

Their radio buzzed again; Ben immediately took the call this time. The person on the other end was shouting, saying the UFO had crashed close to the helicopter's position.

The city's military commander was ordering the pilots to the impact site to investigate.

They arrived a minute later.

They'd expected to see a huge smoldering crater—but this had been no ordinary crash. Whatever the object was, it had come in level, tearing up at least a mile of terrain in the process and creating a deep, black trench sizzling with flaming debris.

They brought the helicopter down to one hundred feet and followed the trench. At its end, they found not a flying saucer, meteorite, or a piece of space junk.

At the end of the trench was . . . a space shuttle.

"This *can't* be!" Ben exclaimed. "There *are* no more space shuttles . . . there haven't been since . . . "

"I hear you," JT interrupted. "But look at it—what else can it be?"

They hovered just above the smoking spacecraft. The size, the shape—there was no doubt it was a space shuttle. But strangely, it was still pretty much in one piece, hinting at a controlled-crash landing.

Then, viewing the wreck through their night-vision goggles, Ben and JT saw movement inside.

Slumped in the pilot's seat, surrounded by smoke and flames, a bleeding, smoldering figure was gamely trying to undo his safety harness.

"Someone *lived* through this?" JT gasped.

"Goddamn, it looks that way."

JT didn't hesitate. He put the helicopter down on top of the spacecraft, set the controls to idle, and immediately jumped out. Ben followed close behind. Suddenly, they were standing in a whirlwind of smoke, steam, and fiery sparks. The thunderstorm was still going full blast.

The pilots had to shout over the noise. "I don't see any kind of a hatch," JT yelled. "Do you?"

The spacecraft began shuddering. The wet, smoky air became thick with the odor of leaking fuel. Ben and JT knew what that meant. The shuttle was going to blow up at any moment.

"Whoever's inside, we gotta get him out right now!" Ben yelled.

Again JT didn't hesitate. He ran back to the copter, retrieved its weapons box, and extracted a shaped charge. Setting it in place, he took out his side arm and shot one round into it.

Ben had barely enough time to duck before the charge went off with a mighty *boom!* The smoke quickly blew away, revealing a jagged hole on the top of the wrecked spacecraft.

"Christ! Give me a little warning will you?" Ben yelled.

But JT didn't hear him. He was already climbing down through the hole.

Ben quickly joined him. They found themselves in a darkened, smoke-filled chamber, wreckage all around them.

Turning their night goggles to full power, they could see the weak light of the flight deck about fifteen feet ahead. The person they'd spotted was still moving around, but not as much as before, as if life was draining out of him.

The spacecraft shuddered again. The stink of heated fuel once more engulfed the copter pilots.

"We gotta move fast, brother," Ben said.

But again JT was already in motion. He began picking his way through the debris separating them from the flight deck.

Ben followed him, but it was hard work, especially in the smoky darkness. Then the spacecraft shook again, and this time, they were nearly overcome by the steaming fumes.

"We've got maybe thirty seconds here!" JT yelled. "Then this thing is going up like a bomb . . . "

They pulled the last piece of debris out of the way and finally clambered up to the flight deck.

The pilot was still strapped into the seat but was no longer moving. He was wearing a thick spacesuit and a helmet, but the suit and the helmet were smoking in multiple places. There was blood on his hands and on the legs and shoulders of the spacesuit.

JT and Ben desperately began cutting through the safety straps, the fumes now clogging their throats. Even if they were able to free the man, they would still have to carry him back to where they'd blasted the opening in the fuselage; boost him up through the hole; get themselves up and then back to the helicopter; and fly away—all before the spacecraft exploded.

And that was just seconds away.

They finally cut through the straps, yanked the pilot out of the seat, and dragged him back to the access hole.

But the hole was five feet over their heads, and the unconscious man seemed too heavy for just one of them to lift. His bloody spacesuit alone must have weighed fifty pounds.

Ben yelled, "How the hell are we going to do this?"

Again, JT simply reacted. He picked up the unconscious man by the shoulders, screaming at Ben to pick him up by the boots. It was awkward and unsteady, but somehow they were able to push him up and out of the hole.

Then JT, the taller of the two, boosted Ben up through the opening as well. Ben had never seen his friend display such strength. The spacecraft shook again, the most vicious tremor of all. The sound of hot gas rushing through the wreck became deafening.

That's when Ben reached down, grabbed JT by the arm, and, displaying some great strength, pulled his friend out of the spacecraft.

They dragged the man to the Huey, threw him inside, then jumped in themselves. They didn't bother strapping in; JT just grabbed the collective and hit the throttles. The copter went straight up into the storm.

Three seconds later the spacecraft blew up.

The blast was so powerful it hurled the copter up another hundred feet before JT regained control.

But he wisely continued the murderous ascent for the next half minute, finally outrunning the flames, smoke, and massive concussion.

Only then were they able to devote attention to their unconscious passenger.

"Is that guy even alive?" JT yelled, exhausted from the rescue effort.

Ben climbed into the back of the helicopter, where the lifeless body lay. He managed to turn the man over and reach under his helmet for a pulse. He found one, but it was weak.

"He's still with us," Ben yelled back to JT. "But not for long."

With some difficulty, Ben unfastened the man's helmet visor and rolled it up.

He saw the man's face and gasped.

"I don't believe this . . . " he yelled over the roar of the copter and the storm. "I don't *fucking* believe this . . . "

JT took a moment from wrestling with the controls to look back at the rear compartment.

"What are you talking about?" he yelled.

But Ben just shook his head, still kneeling over the unconscious body.

JT yelled again. "What the fuck is going on?"

Ben finally looked up, pointed to the man lying on the cabin floor, and said just two words: "It's him . . . "

CHAPTER 2

Football City

THE OLD HUEY LANDED on the roof of Football City's military hospital ten minutes later.

A small army was waiting for it. Medics, nurses, soldiers.

The helipad's landing lights cut brightly through the ferocious rain, illuminating the chaos on the roof. Word about who the injured person on board the copter might be had reached the hospital. But it seemed impossible, too good to be true.

The helicopter was barely down when a half-dozen medics ran forward. Ben pulled back the rear door and the unconscious man was lifted out and placed on a gurney.

The medics rushed him across the windswept helipad, through the nearest doorway, and headlong down the hallway. Running alongside was a team of nurses. Some were trying to take the man's pulse, others were trying to cut away his spacesuit and remove his helmet. But the spacesuit was still smoldering and his helmet proved impossible to get off.

Still, they were all thinking the same thing: *Could it really be him?*

The medics reached the hospital's intensive-care emergency unit and wheeled the gurney inside.

A group of doctors was waiting. They were experts in treating combat wounds from working on Football City soldiers hurt in the city's numerous low-level military actions. Once known as St. Louis, Missouri, Football City was now surrounded by enemies. Fragmented states, criminal enclaves, and outlaw territories formed its borders. Firefights were a daily occurrence. The most seriously wounded soldiers were taken to this ICEU.

But as heroic as those soldiers were, none had created the buzz this patient was generating.

The ICEU doctors began working on him, dousing his spacesuit with water and cutting away the chest area. At that moment, a man in an all-white military uniform arrived. Louis St. Louis, military commander of Football City, was tall, had a shock of gray hair and a ruddy complexion.

He approached the gurney just as the mystery man's helmet was finally lifted off. St. Louis saw the man's face—and suddenly had to sit down. Even the hard-line military doctors gasped in astonishment.

St. Louis looked up at them. "Am I dreaming this?"

One doctor replied, "If you are, then we all are . . . "

The doctors went back to work. Shocking though his presence was, the man in the spacesuit was still seriously injured and needed attention immediately.

The assisting nurses couldn't help themselves. They stole glances over their shoulders at the anxious group of coworkers waiting on the other side of the ICEU's glass wall.

Finally one nurse mouthed the words everyone on the other side of the glass wanted to hear: "It's *really* him . . . "

News traveled quickly. Through the hospital, then over to the adjacent military base, and, from there, to the city streets beyond.

Within minutes, a crowd was gathering outside the hospital.

They'd heard it was nothing short of a miracle. That a man lying in the hospital's ICEU was none other than the long-lost savior of the American continent . . . Hawk Hunter.

But this was impossible.

The Wingman had been dead for years.

CHAPTER 3

HAWK HUNTER WAS LAST SEEN more than a decade ago, climbing aboard a Zon spacecraft, the crude Russian version of America's space shuttle.

Blasting off into outer space, his mission was to track down the super criminal Viktor, who was reportedly holed up in orbit, using the old Russian Mir space station as his base. Just about everything bad that had happened to America since the Big War could be laid at Viktor's cloven feet, which was why people considered him to be Satan incarnate. Hunter had fought him many times before and had hoped the trip to space would be their final battle.

In the midst of this pursuit, a giant comet was spotted heading toward Earth. Moments before humanity would have been obliterated, Hunter took the Zon and waylaid the comet by detonating a trail of nuclear mines in its path. Though he saved the planet, Hunter was killed in mid-space by the massive explosion.

Or, so everyone thought.

To say Hunter, dead or alive, was an American hero was a vast understatement.

He'd attained icon status in the dark days following World War III, a vicious conflict the United States had won on the European battlefield, only to be undermined by the traitorous US vice president, who, proving to be a Russian mole, took down the nation's ballistic missile–defense system just long enough for Russian ICBMs to obliterate the middle of the American heartland.

Though his country was beaten and defenseless, Hunter was able to put together a military force called the United Americans, and eventually won back the homeland from an assortment of enemies, including Russians, neo-Nazis, and Asian warrior cults, as well as armies of homegrown fascists, many of whom had infiltrated America's National Guard.

It had been a remarkable achievement for a man regarded by friend and foe alike as the best fighter pilot who'd ever lived. It was well known that Hunter didn't just fly airplanes; he became one with them. His brain overrode their flight computers; his arms and legs became their ailerons and elevators. He could fly higher and faster than any man alive—and in battle he was absolutely fearless. In the old days, any fighter pilot who shot down five enemy airplanes was considered an ace. Hunter had shot down *hundreds* of enemy airplanes. The skill and bravery he showed in aerial combat was also displayed on the ground, as he proved to be a superb tactician and military strategist.

He was also known to be extremely lucky. So when he climbed into the Zon spacecraft ten years ago, many were sure he'd simply return to Earth shortly afterward with the super-criminal Viktor in tow.

Later, when it was thought that Hunter had died sacrificing himself to save the planet, no one was surprised.

Once Hunter went missing, the American continent quickly reverted back to the dark old days following World War III.

In his absence, the country's old enemies surged back into action, starting a string of small wars that eventually raged from coast to coast. Once again, these battles broke up United America into a collection of fractured states and warring territories, nearly all of them supported by hostile foreign powers.

Football City had suffered badly in this downturn. Named for the nonstop football game that had been played there 24 hours a day, 365 days a year, solely for the purposes of gambling, it had once been considered a shining example of rebirth in postwar America. Now it was a dark, dirty, and depressing place. Crime was rampant. Security was nonexistent. And due to the huge payments it was forking over to one of its particularly belligerent neighbors as "protection money," the city was also quite broke. Those same words could be used to describe America as well.

This was why people were so excited by the rumors that Hunter was alive and suddenly back in Football City.

But was that really what was happening? Football City's top military intelligence officers were on their way to the hospital. The number one question they wanted answered was: Who *is* this person lying in the ICEU?

If it really was Hunter, where had he been all this time?

And if it wasn't him, who was it?

CHAPTER 4

DESPITE THE RAIN, the crowd grew larger around the Football City military hospital as the night wore on.

Word had continued to spread rapidly, causing more and more people to venture out of their homes and into the sodden darkness to the base to see if what everyone was saying was true.

Because most of the streetlights in Football City didn't work anymore, the crowd had started fires in old trashcans. They lit candles and kept them sheltered from the rain, creating a watery glow that could be seen for miles. They waited for any sign that the person lying in a room on the top floor of the hospital was really their long-lost hero.

The atmosphere inside the ICEU had grown more expectant as well. The military doctors had brought the mystery man's pulse back up to an acceptable rate. His heart was stabilized; his oxygen levels had risen. While he had dozens of wounds and burns all over his body, none seemed life threatening, and many had been treated.

Still, the ICEU doctors had called for a combat burns surgeon to check over the patient before they completely cut away his bulky space suit.

In the meantime, Football City's top military intelligence people had arrived and were studying the man as best they could. Six feet tall; ruggedly handsome; blond, rock-star hair; deep-blue eyes—he certainly *looked* like Hawk Hunter. And there was no doubt he'd arrived in a spacecraft that looked a lot like the Zon, although all that was left of it were bits of burnt dust and metal.

But could this be a ruse of some kind? A fake Hunter sent by an enemy for some reason? Anything was possible these dark days. But again, Football City was a mere shadow of its former self. It was combat-weary and being bled dry. Why would one of its enemies attempt such an elaborate hoax? And to what end?

All of this would be settled if the man could talk, but he still hadn't regained consciousness. This puzzled the doctors. None of his vital signs indicated a coma, nor was there any outward evidence that he'd suffered a traumatic brain injury.

He just wasn't conscious—almost as if he was asleep. Or more accurately, in a very deep sleep.

As the doctors were moving their mystery patient to the CAT-scan room to check his brain functions, he suddenly came to life, sitting up on the gurney, startling doctors and nurses alike.

His eyes were wide open, his face full of color. He was looking around, appearing more befuddled than frightened by his surroundings and all the people around him.

Then something came over him. Those who were there would later say it was almost a glow from his head to his feet. His eyes became so intense his irises turned dark. He clenched his fists with so much force he reopened the wounds on his hands, at the same time displaying muscular arms through his ripped space suit. He appeared to be over his confusion.

Suddenly, he seemed to know *exactly* where he was and what was going on—and what he had to do.

Military Commander Louis St. Louis had just arrived back on the scene. Now the mystery man looked him straight in the eye, maybe because St. Louis was the only face in the crowd he recognized, and said in a calm voice, "Something . . . is coming."

With that, the man jumped off the gurney, retrieved his battered helmet resting underneath, and put it back on. When two of the doctors tried to stop him, he gently but firmly resisted their efforts. There were also a dozen soldiers in the hallway looking on. Many of them remembered Hunter from years before; some had even fought alongside him. They simply froze in place.

What was he doing?

The answer came an instant later when Football City's air-raid sirens started going off. Some were so close by that their wailing shook the walls of the hospital.

The man in the space suit cocked his ear skyward, then looked back at St. Louis, and said, "See what I mean?"

Then he began running. Down the hall, into a stairwell, down the stairs. Knocked back to reality, the doctors started yelling at the soldiers: "Go get him!"

But the man was too quick for them. Down ten flights of stairs in a flash, he burst out of an exit door, which put him on the tarmac of Football City's main air base.

He started running again, heading for a handful of jet fighters parked near the base's main runway. The planes made up the bulk of Football City's ragged air corps. Each was more than three quarters of a century old.

In the distance, the air raid sirens continued to bellow. The city's scramble pilots, those few fliers who were on call twenty-four hours a day, valiantly trying to defend the city from its frequent air raids, were running out to the airplanes as well. The pilots saw the mystery man sprint past them, still dressed in his half-burned flight suit and battered crash helmet. In the murky darkness, they didn't know who he was. They watched, dumbfounded as he reached one of the airplanes and climbed in.

He quickly started the jet fighter's engine, and without taking time to let it warm up or to acclimate himself to the cockpit, the man popped the brakes and the elderly warplane moved down the runway.

As the scramble pilots looked on in amazement, the jet fighter rolled right past them and, with a burst of fire from its tail, took off into the stormy night.

The formation of twelve heavy bombers heading for Football City had taken off from a base just forty miles away.

They belonged to a criminal group known as the 10th Street Crew. A coalition of armed gangs that made money enforcing extortion payments, the Crew took its orders from the Red Army Mafia (RAM), the giant organized-crime family that controlled Detroit.

Football City had been paying RAM 50 percent of the city's meager income per month just on the promise that they would not invade. Whenever that payment was late, which was often, RAM called in the 10th Street Crew to do their thing.

The pilots of those dozen bombers were all mercenaries, fly-boys for hire, in the employ of the 10th Street Crew. Assigned to do a dumb-bomb drop on Football City's already battered harbor, many had flown that mission before, with virtual impunity—and there was nothing Football City could do about it.

Just as the formation of bombers appeared on the horizon, though, the storm clouds that had blanketed Football City seemingly for forever began to clear away.

Suddenly, stars could be seen above the city—and, flying in chevrons of three, their navigation lights burning brightly, the oncoming bombers could be seen too.

They made an odd collection. Six were old Russian-built Backfire bombers; two were Tu-95 Bears, also Russian built. There was a trio of extremely old French-built Mirage bombers, and one very out-of-place, British-built, delta-winged Vulcan bomber.

However old they were, many of the bombers stayed on

auto-pilot during their bomb runs because the raids over Football City were so uneventful. Football City's antiaircraft batteries were so antiquated and so few in number, they didn't pose
any kind of threat to the mercenary airmen.

And not once since these bombing missions began had
Football City employed any kind of defensive fighter strategy
that the bomber pilots had to worry about. The bombers were
all supersonic or close to it. The old Football City air fleet flew
only subsonic planes. By the time Football City's fighters could
get started up, get in the air, and then in a position to attack, the
bombers would already have dropped their loads and would be
heading back home at high speed.

Since the clouds had cleared away (miraculously, some would
later say), hundreds of people on the ground had a near-perfect
view of what happened next.

All those people gathered outside the air base fence, plus
dozens more inside the gloomy Football City military headquarters nearby, all the security personnel throughout the
facility, and even the doctors from the hospital who were now
standing on its roof saw the same thing: the bombers approaching from one direction and the lone jet fighter piloted by the
mystery man approaching from the other.

Though very old, the plane he was flying—an F-86 Sabre
jet, built in the early 1950s—was easy to see because he had
it at full throttle, causing a long trail of fiery exhaust to shoot
out of its tail. Yet the enemy pilots never saw him coming.
Facing the dull glow of their target, they could not see his
exhaust in the glare. But more importantly, he'd taken off
and climbed so quickly, he'd never even registered on their
radars.

The seconds ticked away and finally the lights in the sky
merged. With astonishing agility, the little plane dove right
into the bomber formation, its engine screaming. Bright-yellow
lights erupted from its wings, machine guns firing madly at the

enemy. Red streaks flashed across the sky—tracer rounds seeking targets in the flock of bombers.

Suddenly one of the Backfires was on fire. It rolled over on its back and then went straight down, hitting the Mississippi River with a tremendous *crash!* The witnesses on the ground were stunned at how quickly it happened. No sooner had it hit the water when another Backfire exploded in midair. There was no wreckage to crash to Earth this time—just a bright puff of smoke, blown away by the wind. Then a Bear had its wing shot off, right at the root. It too plunged straight down, hitting the water with an enormous, fiery splash.

Then came another midair explosion—another Backfire was gone. The second Bear had its tail blown off, soon joining its brother in a death dive. The Vulcan bomber disappeared in another puff of smoke. Then came a trio of midair explosions—and suddenly the three Mirages were gone.

Nine enemy planes, destroyed in a matter of seconds.

It was at that moment that Football City's antiaircraft crews, momentarily unaware of what was going on above them, opened up with as much fury as they could muster.

The three remaining attackers broke formation in an effort to get away—but the fighter jet pursued them, still firing without mercy. Not only did every shot from the Sabre seem to hit something vital on the bombers, but antiaircraft bursts were going off all around them too.

Finally, even the AA gunners became aware of what was going on—it was impossible not to see the Sabre jet firing, twisting, firing again. It was moving so fast at times, it was little more than a blur.

In all, the incredible and deadly aerial ballet lasted only three minutes. The man flying the Sabre did not give up until all the bombers were shot down, their wreckage strewn along the empty streets near Football City's docks or at the bottom of the Mississippi.

Then everything was quiet. The antiaircraft batteries

stopped firing. The air raid sirens stopped blaring. Through it all, the Football City Air Force never got off the ground.

Still, not a single bomb had been dropped on the city.

The Sabre jet circled the air base once and then came down for a textbook landing.

As it taxied to its hardstand, the people standing outside the base's fence gave a hearty cheer. They'd seen what the jet had done—and though they could hardly believe it, for the first time in a long time, the 10th Street Crew's bombers had not destroyed part of their beloved-if-grimy city.

The Sabre jet finally rolled to a stop. Its engine quickly shut down and its canopy popped open. An access ladder appeared and was put against the fuselage.

St. Louis bounded up the steps, realizing with some horror that the Sabre jet was perforated with hundreds of holes, received not from the attacking bombers, but from friendly fire coming from Football City's game, but wildly inaccurate, anti-aircraft batteries.

St. Louis reached the top of the ladder just as the pilot was taking off his battered crash helmet. The man looked up at St. Louis and said, "Did I really just do that?"

St. Louis didn't reply. He couldn't—he was too choked up. His city had been spared, at least for tonight, and he owed it all to this man.

He finally allowed the ground crew personnel to take over and help the pilot out of the heavily damaged Sabre jet. By that point, a number of Football City's military leaders had gathered near the plane.

As they watched the mystery man being placed back on a stretcher and wheeled back to the military hospital, St. Louis turned to them and smiled through his tears.

"There's no doubt in my mind now," he said. "That man is Hawk Hunter."

PART TWO

THE UNIVERSE NEXT DOOR

CHAPTER 5

One week later

HUNTER WAS VERY UNCOMFORTABLE lying on the couch.

It was too short for his six-foot frame and felt like it was stuffed with rocks. Squirming did him no good. He just couldn't find the right position to get comfortable and settle down.

Sitting close by, pen and pad in hand, was Football City's most preeminent—and only—psychiatrist. The questions had been coming nonstop for the past half hour.

What is your earliest memory? Did your parents love you? Why do you think you have this compulsion to fly? Why do you always carry your helmet around with you?

Hunter answered as best he could. His memory had cleared, somewhat, just as he was landing the Sabre jet after shooting down the twelve enemy bombers a week before. He knew his name, knew where he was born, knew when he'd started flying. He remembered World War III and the feeling of being stabbed in the back when the quisling vice president allowed the center of the country to be nuked. He remembered the nightmare of the aftermath.

He remembered a lot of it—but not all of it. He knew who Ben, JT, and St. Louis were right away, but other names and faces just weren't coming to him. And while he remembered blasting off in the Zon spacecraft more than ten years ago, what happened after that was entirely fuzzy.

That's why he was there, on the shrink's couch, at St. Louis's suggestion. If he could unlock the rest of his memory, he might be able to explain how he'd survived in space after the big comet explosion and where he'd been in the interim.

But it wasn't only this blank memory or the barrage of questions that was making him squirm.

The psychiatrist was making him a little jumpy as well.

When St. Louis first suggested he visit the shrink, Hunter imagined some dour old guy with a tweed jacket and a pipe.

He couldn't have been more wrong.

The shrink was an incredibly beautiful woman. As soon as he'd walked into her office, Hunter couldn't take his eyes off her. She was brunette, shapely, well dressed. As he lay down on the couch, she closed the window shades and placed her chair very close to him, so close that out of the corner of his eye he could see her beautiful legs and one of her high heels dangling just inches above the floor.

Even when he wasn't peeking, he could smell her perfume and could feel her electricity, her warm breath as it touched his cheek.

There were no brain lapses here—his nucleus accumbens was firing just fine. She was so gorgeous that he was just plain nervous.

Their session was supposed to last an hour, but about forty minutes in, she abruptly put down her pen and pad.

She moved her chair even closer to him, if that was possible.

"I think we've got a good start here," she told him in a soft voice. "A door has been opened. More memories might flow if we can find a trigger to release them."

"What kind of trigger?" he asked.

She thought a moment, then said, "Well, some research suggests that a extraordinary physical experience opens the amygdala in the brain and helps retrieve lost memories."

"What kind of 'extraordinary physical experience'? I mean, I had a hell of an experience my first night here."

"Everyone knows that," she told him. "And we haven't been bombed since, and frankly, I appreciate the quiet nights. But for you, I was thinking of something more personal. More tactile."

"Please don't write this down," he said. "But I think I'm a little confused . . . "

She laughed. "When was the last time you had a sensual physical experience?"

Hunter thought for a moment. "I think that's one of the things I can't remember."

She laughed again and then purred, "Maybe we can do something about that."

"Really? Like what?"

He looked up and saw that she was unbuttoning her blouse. Her hair came down next, then her glasses disappeared. If possible, she looked even more beautiful than before.

She held up a gold watch and began swinging it in front of his eyes.

"You're hypnotizing me?" he asked.

"Think of it more as a relaxation exercise," she said. "Let the thoughts come, no matter how unusual they might be."

She was leaning right over him now, so close that her open blouse was touching his face.

But he did as he was told, watching the gold watch go back and forth. Back and forth. Back . . . and forth

His eyes closed and he felt like he was floating. Then his head was filled with the oddest thoughts. First, he saw a huge sequoia tree sprouting out of the ground. Then, a hot dog with legs, chasing a donut, also with legs.

Then, finally, a train going into a tunnel.

Ben and JT were waiting in the psychiatrist's outer office.

Of all the people Hunter had fought with, they were his closest friends. Even before World III, they'd all flown together in the US Air Force's Aerial Demonstration Team, better known as the Thunderbirds.

Then, after the Big War, they became the core of the United Americans Air Force and were at Hunter's side through many battles, big and small. That they were the ones who had rescued him from the burning Zon was one of the strangest aspects of his bizarre return to Earth.

It was also strange that he looked exactly the same to them. He hadn't aged. His hair hadn't changed. No graying, no paunch. They'd joked that wherever he went, he must have found the fountain of youth.

The shrink's office was in one of the better parts of Football City, one of the few remaining. But as it didn't have a helipad on the roof, Hunter had been forced to use ground transport to get there.

This presented somewhat of a problem. Since his return, Hunter had become a major celebrity, with crowds gathering daily outside his quarters in the Football City Military Building, and following him just about everywhere he went. Even a brief wave from his window could send the crowds into a frenzy, especially the females.

For his own protection, he'd spent most of the last week holed up in his two-room officer's apartment, talking with Ben and JT and writing down everything he could remember.

On those rare occasions he went out, they served as his bodyguards.

The door to the shrink's office opened and Hunter half-stumbled out. His hair was mussed, his flight suit was askew, and he had the same befuddled look he'd had the night he'd arrived in Football City.

"What the hell were you doing in there?" Ben asked him. "Wrestling?"

Hunter shrugged. "Something like that."

JT called down to the street to make sure Hunter's security

team was in place and that a vehicle was waiting. When the reply came back affirmative, he and Hunter started down the stairs. At that moment, the shrink came out of her office. She was also slightly disheveled.

She signaled to Ben that she wanted to talk to him.

"He's a fascinating case, in more ways than one," she said, fixing her hair.

"Any advice you can give us?" Ben asked.

She put her glasses back on.

"I think these lost memories will come back on their own now," she said. "You can remind him of things or events or people, but only if he brings up the subject first. In other words, don't force him to remember anything or anybody. Just let the memories return naturally."

Ben shrugged. "You're the expert."

She shook her head. "Actually, not in this case. From what I know about him, and a bit of what he's told me—well, let's just say there are things there that go beyond my range of experience."

She took a business card from her pocket.

"I heard of a secret government project years ago when I was a grad student," she said. "It was before the Big War. A research team looking into anomalies. I mean, *real* anomalies. They were investigating strange things that had happened mostly to the military. Things that no one could explain. It went into limbo sometime after the Big War—I'm not sure when. But the first guy to head the project is a local."

She wrote some information on the back of her card and handed it to him.

"Maybe you can have your rock-star friend talk to him," she suggested. "He might be able to help in a way I can't."

Ben took the card and thanked her.

As he was leaving, she called out to him, "Just make sure he's back in time for our session next week."

CHAPTER 6

The next day

THE TRIO OF HELICOPTERS circled the mountaintop home once before landing.

They were all Hueys, the entire complement of Football City's rotary corps. Two were modestly outfitted as gunships, and the third was the same aged eggbeater that Ben and JT had used to rescue Hunter from his burning spacecraft. All three were riding in it once again.

Their copter touched down last and Hunter started to climb off. But JT caught him by the arm.

"Hang tight," JT told him. "We gotta make sure the area is secure. St. Louie's orders."

Hunter sat back down and waited while JT, Ben, and the crews from the other two copters checked out the site.

They didn't have much to scour. The house was built atop the tallest hill in what used to be the state of Missouri. About one hundred miles west of Football City in an otherwise-unoccupied territory, the hill was barely five hundred feet high and its summit was a half acre at best.

The house itself was an A-frame design made almost entirely of glass, perfect for appreciating the impressive view. But there were no security guards, no security cameras. The person who lived in the house lived alone.

Ben and JT gave Hunter the thumbs-up. He stepped out of the copter and stretched. Though he hated being treated like a celebrity, he knew St. Louis was just looking out for him. Besides, Hunter was suddenly a very valuable commodity; his skill alone had saved Football City for at least one night—and maybe more. Neither the 10th Street Crew nor Red Army Mafia had been heard from since he'd shot their bombers out of the sky. St. Louis hadn't sent the criminals their monthly vig either, and still, not a peep. Maybe RAM was thinking over its options, but for sure, the Crew had gotten the message.

The front door to the A-frame was open and a man was standing in the doorway. He was middle aged, slightly built with long, gray hair, and a long, gray beard. His name was Dr. Pott.

He greeted Hunter warmly. "I never thought I'd get to meet the great Hawk Hunter," he said, shaking the pilot's hand enthusiastically.

"I'm as surprised as you are," Hunter replied.

Dr. Pott had worked as an intelligence analyst for the US government before the Big War. While, officially, he'd been assigned to the Air Force's Advanced Weapons Section, in reality he'd led a classified project called AII (Anomalous Incident Investigation).

At its height, AII contained a dozen scientists—experts in advanced mathematics, quantum mechanics, and string theory—with a like number of military intelligence people. Their orders were to look into truly anomalous events, many of which were related to military aviation, that the US government had deemed security issues. The group was considered so secret that even the location of its facility was classified.

While AII disappeared sometime after the Big War, Pott had left long before, sequestering himself on his hill, surviving on homegrown vegetables, MREs, and apparently, cannabis. His house reeked, ironically, of pot.

He and Hunter sat down in a spacious living room, the view of the prairie spread out before them. Ben and JT joined them while the rest of the copter contingent set up a defense perimeter outside.

Pott explained that having read the classified documents St. Louis had sent him about what happened the night Hunter arrived, he now believed that Hunter's sudden appearance definitely qualified as an anomalous event as defined by his old AII research project.

"There have been a number of cases over the years that no one can explain," Pott told them. "Things that are just different from what we'd call 'normal.' "

He took out a pipe, casually packed it with marijuana, lit it, and took an enormous drag. He offered it to his guests, but they all declined.

"For example," Pott went on, letting out a huge cloud of smoke, "in early 1909, years before the first war in which a Zeppelin was used, people in England saw strange airships flying overhead; they called them Scareships. In 1934, people in Sweden reported seeing enormous airplanes with large wings, up to ten engines, and giant floats underneath that were unlike any airplane ever built. In the summer of 1946, again over Sweden, people saw mysterious rockets flying in formation, taking ninety-degree turns, displaying flight characteristics way ahead of the times. No one ever figured out what any of these things were. They all just seemed of a different technology, from a different time or place.

"And all those UFO crashes that became popular? Roswell? Aztec, New Mexico? Kecksburg, Pennsylvania? The AII treated them not as extraterrestrial events, but more like technology that was not of the time. Put in that perspective, these things make a little more sense scientifically.

"I ran the AII project for a few years and saw enough to know there was something very strange going on—especially in cases with a lot of documented proof. It was all very bizarre. In fact, the only hypothesis we even considered was the multiverse theory."

Pott saw three blank expressions staring back at him.

"You know, the idea that what we call the universe might actually be just one of an infinite number of universes?" he said. "And in some of these universes, everything might be the same, except for a slight difference here and there?"

Again, three blank stares.

"Okay, let's try this example," he said. "Maybe in some other universe close by, the Scareships were actually war Zeppelins that were developed years earlier than in this universe. Or maybe in another universe, someone actually built ten-engine airplanes that flew over Sweden or cruise missiles forty years ahead of their time. Or maybe that the mode of air transportation in the universe next door isn't airplanes but brightly colored, saucer-shaped flying discs.

"Because string theory says that these separate universes would have to be infinite in number, then every possible scenario you can think of must be true. A universe where red is green and vice versa. A universe where cigarettes are good for you, and fruits and veggies are deadly. A universe where the South Pole is just one-millionth degree warmer than the South Pole we know. In most cases, we're all the same, and everything else is all the same, just with these little divergences. I know it sounds crazy, but the only theory that could explain the phenomena we were studying was that maybe, on rare occasions, objects can pass between separate universes."

Hunter asked the question on everyone's minds: "But what does this have to do with me?"

"Well, it just follows that maybe people can pass between universes as well," Pott replied. "For example, we investigated a jet fighter that disappeared over Lake Superior in 1953. It was chasing a UFO at the time. The jet's radar blip and that of the UFO merged, and then the combined blip just disappeared. The plane's wreckage was never found, the pilots' bodies never recovered. Where did they go? No one knows. But our hypothesis said they might have passed through to another universe. That case reminds me of yours, Major Hunter. And the fact that the plane was chasing a UFO makes it that much more intriguing."

Pott took another drag of his pipe.

"It's all just conjecture," he began again, blowing out another cumulus cloud of smoke. "But after reading about your case, I think it's possible you, Major Hunter, may have somehow jumped from one universe to another. You might have come from a place that was just a little different from this one. Just a little ahead or a little behind. But you did most of the same things in both, had the same friends and so on."

Hunter was trying mightily to keep an open mind, but all the pot smoke was a bit distracting. In fact, he was getting a contact high.

"Let's assume all that is true," he said. "Then why can I remember some things and not others? I mean, I know some of what happened to me before I got into the Zon. But not all. And not anything that happened afterward. Why would that be?"

"It's simple . . . maybe," Pott said, taking another puff. "The theory says that if you are passing through universes, you're also moving through time. The different universes aren't necessarily synced up. They are probably going along on their own timelines. Many might be a nanosecond off, but others could be off by thousands or even millions of years.

"In your instance, now that you've returned, it seems that you have some of the same memories as your friends—but not quite all and not quite the same. For instance, they remember your blasting off in the Zon alone, but you seem to think you were with some of your allies. They remember your diverting the comet, yet you have no memory of what happened after the Zon took off. See? It almost proves the theory. Little things are different in each universe. Maybe in one universe, there is no comet. Maybe in another, you divert the comet, and it becomes another moon, orbiting the Earth. Maybe in a third, despite your best efforts, the comet hits the Earth, and we go the way of the dinosaurs. The possibilities are literally infinite.

"So wherever you were these past ten years after you took off in the Zon, maybe the timeline of those memories just hasn't caught up with you yet. Until then, you'll remember some things, and then bits and pieces of other things, and then maybe, for some things, not at all."

There was a long silence in the room. It was a lot to take in.

"Where did this AII research take place?" JT finally asked.

The doctor took a long toke and exhaled. "We were working out at Groom Lake," he said casually.

Like the cloud of smoke, his words hung in the air for a moment.

"Groom Lake?" Ben asked. "You mean . . . Area 51?"

The doctor nodded. "The one and only. UFOs. Aliens. Bigfoot. Elvis. They were all out there somewhere, though, I can tell you, all very well hidden. It seemed like the perfect place to study multiverse theory. In fact, after I left, I heard they were trying to find a way to 'jump' between universes, just as you might have jumped, Major Hunter.

"The deep scuttlebutt said they'd already been able to retrieve objects from 'other places' somehow—and that they had some of these retrieved objects in storage out there, along with a lot of data and research."

He took one long last puff on his pipe and added, "There might even be a file on you out there, Major Hunter. I know some of my colleagues hung on to the project after the Big War and stayed at Groom Lake for as long as they could. Who knows what they came up with?"

They left soon afterward, taking off from the mountaintop in a burst of dust and exhaust.

Heading back to Football City, Hunter was deep in thought. JT and Ben also stayed quiet.

Finally, Hunter said, "Well, what did you think?"

Both friends shrugged.

"Of Dr. Pott?" JT asked. "He's got the right name."

Ben nodded in agreement. "The guy's obviously baked 24/7. Who knows what's real, and what's coming out of that pipe?"

Hunter nodded. "I know I have to take it all with a grain of salt, but from where I'm standing, I've got nothing else."

His friends anticipated his next thought.

"If only we could get to Area 51," Hunter continued, "find this AII place, get inside, see what's there, see what those guys left behind."

Ben took a deep breath. "Hawk, that part of Nevada is under the control of the Asian Mercenary Cult," he said. "Do you remember them?"

Hunter did—but vaguely.

"We fought them tooth and nail way back when," JT said. "Had to go across the Pacific to kick their ass. But they're like lice: they don't go away."

Ben explained, "These days, the AMC controls a large part of the American Southwest, including Las Vegas, which is still open and providing lots of capital for them. They're also in Los Angeles and down in San Diego."

Ben paused for a moment and then said, "Sorry, Hawk, but that research facility is deep inside enemy territory."

CHAPTER 7

HUNTER WAS BACK in his quarters an hour later.

The sun was going down, and as he looked out of his tenth-floor window, he could see more than a few streetlights popping on, another sign that Football City was coming back to life.

The crowd below had not dissipated. In fact, it looked larger. He gave a quick wave, heard the cheers from below, and then moved away from the window for the night.

A knock at the door brought a pretty female orderly bearing a small bag. She explained to Hunter that it contained items found on him when he crashed. He thanked her and dumped the bag on his bed. It contained his boots, gloves, and a large combat pistol. But the item that caught and held his attention was a small folded piece of cloth. He studied it closely.

What was it?

Red-and-white stripes, a field of blue covered with stars . . .

Those stars. Those stripes . . .

If Pott was right, there would be some things he'd always remember, some things he might remember, and some things he would never remember at all. That was a heart-wrenching thought, to know that crucial pieces of him were missing, maybe never to be found again.

But then he looked at the small folded flag in his hands and his eyes became misty.

"But this," he whispered, touching the flag to his chest. "At least I remember this . . . "

Ten floors below, JT and Ben were sitting at the bar in Football City's last remaining Officers' Club. It was a dingy place, a far cry from its heyday when Football City was *the* place to be on the American continent.

JT and Ben were the only patrons. They needed scotch. It had been a strange week.

They had spent the last ten years without Hunter to guide them, trying their best to make a living flying anything that could get off the ground. It had been a tough time, because Hunter had always known the right way to go.

But now that he was back, it was like those ten years had never happened. They felt like Peter and Paul again.

Very strange . . .

Hunter appeared out of the shadows and sat down next to Ben. He tried to get the attention of the sleepy bartender.

"What the hell are you doing here?" Ben half-yelled at him.

"Getting a drink," Hunter simply replied.

Ben and JT exchanged expressions of disbelief. They looked out the bar's cracked window at the crowd of Wingman admirers outside.

"Are you insane?" JT scolded Hunter. "If those people see you in here, they'll tear this place apart."

Hunter shrugged. "It could use the renovation," he said, finally getting the bartender's attention. Moments later a huge scotch was set down before him.

He downed it in one massive swig and ordered another.

"Okay, so maybe that guy today was too high or too something," he said, picking up their earlier conversation. "But that doesn't mean everything he told us isn't true. And I don't want to start a war with the Asian Mercenary Cult. That would be unwise at this point. But at the same time, I've got to find out if anything he said was on the level. I'll go nuts if I don't."

"What are you saying?" JT asked.

"Maybe I can go out to Groom Lake myself," Hunter said in a half-whisper. "I can get on the ground, sneak in somehow, and try to find the AII Research Center. I've done stuff like that before—right?"

JT held up his hand. "Hold on, amigo. I'll tell you right now, a one-man show ain't the way to go. The AMC has got to be *all over* the place out there. You'd have to take an army with you, and even then, it could only be a raid. Like a cheap date, in and out . . ."

Hunter signaled the bartender for three more drinks.

"But I *can't* do it that way," he said. "This is *my* problem. I can't expect other people to risk their lives just because I've got a memory block. Plus—"

But again, JT stopped him. "Hawk, like I said, you're not doing anything alone. If you do anything, at the very least we're going with you."

Ben added, "Would it be an uphill climb? Yes. Can we raise an army and move it, what? Fifteen hundred miles? I mean, how do you move ten or fifteen thousand guys that far anyway? In railcars, maybe? And who'll pay for it? I don't know. But we'll figure it out if we have to."

Hunter hung his head. He was faced with two stark options: either get into Area 51 by himself and probably get killed, or start a war with an opponent ten times the size of any armed force he could ever hope to muster . . . and get a lot of his friends killed.

He thought for a long time and finally said, "Well, we can't make a decision until we get some eyes on the place. I don't suppose we have any recon photos of Groom Lake?"

Ben and JT shook their heads no.

"We barely have a working recon camera around here," JT said.

"How about a plane that can fly more than two hundred miles in any direction?" Hunter asked.

"You'd have better luck finding a recon camera," Ben replied.

Hunter drained his drink. "I'd still like a close look at exactly what St. Louis has for airplanes, though—besides the Sabres, I mean."

"It's mostly rust and dust," Ben warned him.

"You never know what might be helpful," Hunter said. "Let's go."

"Go?" JT asked, surprised. "Go where?"

"To the air base," Hunter replied. "Maybe we'll find a jewel in the rough."

Once again they looked out the bar's front window and saw the crowd outside had actually swelled in the last ten minutes.

"How can we go anywhere?" JT asked him. "You'll be mobbed."

Hunter just smiled. "That's what back doors are for."

CHAPTER 8

Five days later

THERE'S A TYPE OF COYOTE that lives in the central part of Nevada called the Ghost Dog. While some insist this animal can appear and disappear at will, its name comes not from any supernatural talent, but from its distinctive howl.

It was that howl, high-pitched and echoing, that Hunter thought he heard in his headphones, even though he was thirteen miles above Earth.

He was behind the controls of a B-57 Canberra, an airplane nearly as old as the Sabre jet he'd used his first night back in Football City.

Originally a British design, the US Air Force built the B-57 in the mid-1950s as a medium bomber. But the plane also had another purpose. With the right modifications, the dual-engine jet could fly both long and high—two capabilities needed for a good reconnaissance plane.

Hunter had been pleasantly surprised to find the B-57 amid the "rust and dust" of Football City's Air Force. It was just what he needed. He'd tinkered with it for a few days, enjoying getting his hands dirty again. Normally the longest range for a B-57 was about twenty-eight hundred miles. Round trip from Football City to Nevada was more like thirty-two hundred. So the lighter Hunter could make the aircraft, the better.

He removed any unnecessary weight and replaced it with extra fuel. This meant all the weaponry had to go—the bomb racks, the backup hydraulic systems, even the second cockpit, where a navigator would normally sit.

For this trip, Hunter would follow the stars.

He also reinforced the new one-man cockpit, bulked up the heater, and made adjustments to the plane's twin engines' fuel-intake valves. With these few tweaks, he managed to increase the plane's maximum altitude to seventy thousand feet, far beyond what he hoped AMC's radar net was set to catch.

With St. Louis's blessing, and with JT and Ben looking on, albeit a bit uneasily, he left Football City in the late afternoon and headed west. Immediately climbing to 70-Angels, , he stayed at just under three hundred miles per hour to save precious fuel.

The sixteen-hundred-mile flight out had been adventure free. The winds had been favorable, and he'd used only half his gas.

Best of all, he arrived just before midnight, the perfect time for this one-man spy mission.

Coming over the Snake Mountains, then the Egan Range, the vast, empty Nevada desert finally stretched before him.

The landscape was mostly unbroken. The only deviations were the occasional mountain range or gully, both of which could run for miles.

But there were no lights anywhere on the ground. Nor was there a moon out. The only illumination Hunter could see, other than his cockpit's old LEDs, was coming from the billions of stars overhead.

He tested the plane's jimmy-rigged recon camera, which had been the only one left in Football City. Attached to the bottom of the B-57's nose, it was old but functional. It included an infrared-zoom lens that he could access from the cockpit, allowing him to focus in on objects on the ground while taking pictures of them.

He knew he was approaching Groom Lake when he saw the barest glow of lights on the horizon. A minute later, he was just a few miles away from the air base.

Activating the camera's zoom function, he got ready to study what was below. Groom Lake had one of the longest runways in the world, so he expected to find rows of AMC fighter planes stretched from one end to the other.

But he was surprised to see from one mile out that the base appeared devoid of any military equipment. There were no airplanes on the long runway, no fuel trucks, no weapons, no personnel. Nor were there any signs of life around the three dozen or so buildings that made up the secret base. Hunter couldn't believe it. He'd just assumed the AMC would be firmly established here.

Except for a few dim lights, Area 51 looked deserted.

But suddenly, as if a lightning bolt had hit him, his whole body shook from head to toe. It was not "the feeling"—the sensation he experienced when airplanes were approaching.

This was different.

This felt more like an ocean wave, washing over him, overwhelming him.

He closed his eyes for a moment—and the memories flooded in . . .

Friends . . . Names . . . Faces . . .

General Seth Jones . . . at one time, he'd been like a father to Hunter. General Dave Jones . . . Seth's twin brother, just as brave, just as heroic. Mike Fitzgerald . . . his old drinking buddy and the soul of the United Americans. Yaz . . . his close pal. Donn Jurjan . . . the spy whose code name was "Lazarus." Geraci. Frost. Cook. Miller. The Cobra Brothers. Captain Crunch. Elvis . . .

Then came the places, so sharp and clear . . . Cumulous clouds over Cape Cod. An aircraft carrier being pulled by tugboats across the Mediterranean. A long train ride across America. Flying like a madman across the Pacific. The heat of the jungles in Vietnam. Lolita Island . . .

Then more names and faces . . . His enemies . . . Viceroy Dick, Duke Devillian, Studs, Colonel Krupp, Hashi Pushi—and, of course, Viktor, the Devil himself.

Thankfully, those distorted images gave way to other faces, soft and beautiful. Emma. Diamond. The devastatingly erotic Elizabeth Sandlake. Chloe . . .

Something went flying by his mind's eye at such great speed that it was just a blur. Then that image faded and another took its place: a foggy airfield at night. Across the runway, a blonde, almost angelic-looking woman was beckoning to him.

Her knew her. Knew her well . . .

That blonde angel . . .

What was her name?

But then it was like someone threw a switch. As soon as he asked *that* question, the memory stream just stopped.

He tried desperately to get it back—but it was no use. The strange sensation had come and gone in a flash and now he was back in the cockpit of the B-57 again, looking down at Area 51 from thirteen miles up.

But one thought stayed with him.

"There's something down there . . ." he heard himself whisper, eyes glued on the secret base. "Something down there just caused that."

Then he shook himself back to reality and forced himself to focus.

That had all been very strange.

But he had a job to do.

He managed to turn south, and a few minutes later, he was approaching the green-and-gold glow of Las Vegas.

He was over it in an instant—but that was enough for him. Las Vegas looked like it was mainlining amphetamines. A multitude of heat signatures were coming up at him, from the dozens of casinos, from hundreds of vehicles in the streets, and from thousands of people, too.

Nothing had changed at the famous gambling mecca. Just as Ben and JT had said, Hunter could almost smell the money at seventy thousand feet.

He turned west and in a few seconds was over his third recon target: the enormous facility once known as Nellis Air Force Base, which was about seventy-five miles away from Groom Lake.

This place had been extremely important to the American military before the Big War. In Hunter's early years, when he was flying with the Thunderbirds, he'd spent a lot of time there.

But looking down on it now, he realized it was the opposite of what he'd just seen at Groom Lake. There were dozens of AMC aircraft below, including many foreign-made, high-tech jet fighters. There was also a huge fuel dump, a massive communications tower, forests of small antennae indicating some kind of an air defense system, and what looked like the opening to a huge underground cavern on the west side of the base.

He could also see lots of lights and lots of body heat throughout the installation. It was obvious Nellis was a very important place for the AMC.

Suddenly his bingo light clicked on. He now had just enough fuel to get back to Football City.

He finally turned east.

His immediate conclusions were unexpected. While Nellis was extremely active—no surprise—and Las Vegas was as brassy as advertised—apart from whatever had caused his strange sensations and flood of memories—Groom Lake appeared dead, deserted, abandoned. Based on what he'd seen, getting into Area 51 might be less complicated than he'd previously thought.

Yes, going in alone was probably as impractical as Ben and JT had warned. But maybe he wouldn't need an entire army either.

Maybe all he'd need was a few versatile airplanes and a few brave souls.

He checked his flight watch and nudged his throttles ahead slightly.

He didn't want to be late for his next appointment with the shrink.

PART THREE

THE BATTLE OF DETROIT

CHAPTER 9

THE DARKEST BACK ALLEYS in Football City were on the east side, right along the river.

Lined with shuttered storefronts and rundown apartment buildings, these alleys were havens for all kinds of illicit activity.

Dressed in dark hoodies and camo fatigues, Hunter, Ben, and JT were walking the alleys, looking for a notorious east-side address.

Getting there had involved yet another small military operation. Ben and JT, in their trusty Huey, had flown Hunter off the roof of the military building around noon, while St. Louis, wearing Hunter's helmet and bomber jacket, stood at the window in Hunter's quarters and waved to the crowds below, distracting them.

Landing next to the Mississippi after a two-minute flight, the trio had pulled their hoodies up tight around their faces and started walking. Hunter had briefly told his friends about his flash of memories the night before, but as the psychiatrist had advised Ben, his friends didn't push the subject. Soon enough they were swallowed up by crowds of similarly dressed people who were going about the business of doing illegal things.

They found the address they were looking for halfway down

a particularly shabby alley. It was a basement flat guarded by two surly gunmen. They snapped to attention, though, when Hunter pulled back his hoodie and showed them his face.

Everyone in Football City knew the Wingman—and everyone had heard about his miraculous return.

"He's expecting us," Hunter told the goons.

The gunmen stepped aside.

He, Ben, and JT went down the stairs and entered a dimly lit room. More hired guns were sitting around a table playing cards. Dealing out the next hand was an elderly man with a shaved head and a long, stringy beard, who was dressed in an ancient disco-era jumpsuit.

Hunter knew him right away.

His name was Roy from Troy.

Hunter had first met Roy in upstate New York a few months after World War III ended. Roy was the biggest arms dealer around at the time, and Hunter was looking for weapons to start the United American armed forces. Roy always came through for Hunter, on time, with good merchandise, and for the right price.

But that had been an eternity ago. Hunter guessed Roy was at least one hundred years old by now.

He walked over and shook the old man's hand. Roy gave Hunter a fatherly pat on the chest.

"I've seen a lot of things in my day," Roy said, his voice a wheeze. "But I never thought I'd see you again."

"Same here, Roy," Hunter replied.

Roy studied him for a moment. "I see you're back in form with the ladies? You have that look about you."

Hunter became flustered, but Roy was right. He'd seen his shrink just two hours before.

"Doctor's orders," was all he could say.

Roy signaled they should sit down. Another wave of his hand brought a round of whiskey.

"So, Hawker, what do you need this time?" Roy asked with a thin smile.

Hunter tasted his whiskey. "We're looking for armed transport to fly to a location about fifteen hundred miles away," he said. "We have to land with a few squads of operators, stay on the ground for a couple hours, and then bug out."

Roy thought a moment. "Level of opposition?"

Hunter shrugged. "Moderate to possibly none."

Roy opened a huge binder in front of him. He went through it slowly, finally stopping at a well-worn page.

"It's a small market," he said. "But maybe something like this?"

He turned the book around so his visitors could see. The page held several photos showing a squadron of two-engine, prop-driven airplanes.

"B-25 Mitchells?" Hunter asked.

Roy nodded. "They're small, versatile. They can carry more than a pilot and crew a fairly long distance, and they're not bad on fuel. Plus they have firepower, if needed. Refit one to haul nothing but gas, and you'd get there and back no problem."

Hunter studied the photos. The Mitchell *was* a great airplane—elderly but great. They were used in World War II for everything from medium bombers to naval attack craft. But with the right modifications, more than a dozen people could ride in one.

And while the B-25 was older than the F-86 Sabre, the line of Mitchells in Roy's photos had obviously been reconditioned. They looked like new airplanes.

St. Louis had told Hunter he would support any plan that would get him to Groom Lake to look for the AII research center. At that moment, Hunter thought these planes were just what he needed.

But there was a problem.

When Hunter asked for their price, Roy just shook his head. "For you, old friend, it would have been a very fair number."

"What do you mean, 'would have been'?" JT asked him impatiently.

"I mean I thought I had bought these beauties just a few days ago," Roy said. "But no sooner did I deliver the asking price when someone stole them."

Hunter frowned. "Who swiped them?"

Roy smiled grimly. "That's the rub."

He showed them another photo. It depicted one of the reconditioned B-25s wearing the markings of the Red Army Mafia.

"They're up in Detroit?" Hunter asked, surprised.

"They are," Roy confirmed. "Along with a lot of other stuff."

Ben and JT got up to go, but Hunter stayed seated. He knew Roy better than they did.

"You wouldn't be telling me all this if there wasn't some point to it," he said.

Roy waved his hand and the gunmen seated at the table got up and left the room.

Once they were gone, he went on, "Hawk, I think it's very opportune that after all these years, you walked into my shop today."

Hunter sipped his drink again. "How so?"

Roy lowered his wheezy voice. "The RAM has been on a bomber-buying spree lately," he said. "Anything with more than one engine that they can't buy, they're stealing. They're trying to keep it secret, but I've been told those mooks are grabbing up every mud mover they can get their hands on. Plus they've bought up just about every aerial bomb in the country too. It's very odd."

"Any idea what it's about?" Hunter asked. Roy shook his head. "I don't know. No one does . . . "

The old man sipped his drink again. "So, Hawk, any suggestions?"

Hunter knew where this was going. "You probably want us to go up to Detroit and snatch those Mitchells back for you."

Roy leaned forward and nodded. "Well, if you did," he said,

"I'd get my revenge, and you could use some of them for your little side mission—free of charge, of course."

JT piped up. "But grabbing those planes back from the RAM? They ain't exactly Cub Scouts you know. We'd stir up a huge shit storm."

No one spoke for a moment. While nowhere near as powerful as the Asian Mercenary Cult, the Red Army Mafia was still bad news. They'd been ruling Detroit with an iron fist for years.

"They have weaknesses," Roy said. "As all devils do. But whatever the case, I think you should look into this whole bomber-buying thing, Hawk. It's such strange behavior on their part. It's troubling. And we all know that back in the old days, you could figure out something like this during breakfast and have it solved by lunch."

Hunter thought a moment, trying to digest the puzzling information.

"We'll see," he told Roy finally. "And if we come up with anything, we'll be in touch."

The old arms dealer smiled again, his eyes lighting up. Then he showed them another photograph. This one was of a warship. "While you're doing your homework on RAM, you might want to consider this."

CHAPTER 10

Later that day

THE CONVERTED B-57 RECON PLANE took off just as the sun was going down.

Hunter was at the controls again, the old infrared camera locked and loaded. He reached seventy thousand feet and quickly turned northeast. It would take him less than ninety minutes to cover the six hundred miles to Detroit.

He was worried. He didn't dare entertain any theories about why RAM was accumulating bombers at such a rapid rate until he got a look at what was going on. That was the reason for this flight.

Before he left, Ben and JT had briefed him further on the Red Army Mafia. A mishmash alliance of Russian mafioso that had come to America just as it was being fractured and decided to stay, it had ruled the rough-and-tumble Motor City for about ten years. Their policies were similar to those of the Asian Mercenary Cult: extort and enslave the population and allow a privileged few to enjoy prosperous lives.

As Hunter recalled, that was about as un-American as one could get.

Time flew by, and Hunter was soon approaching his target.

He clicked on the camera just as he passed above Detroit's outer defense line. Activating the zoom lens, he immediately saw numerous signs of military activity below. Artillery positions, troop trucks, and even tanks watched over key roadways and bridges. RAM seemed to be everywhere.

Soon he was over the Motor City itself, only to see more of the same. Detroit was an armed camp these days—not as protection against any outside forces, but simply as a way of keeping its captive population in line.

He passed over RAM headquarters. Housed in what used to be the world headquarters of General Motors, the former automobile giant, even from thirteen miles up, the seven separate interconnected glass towers looked magnificent. And no surprise, they were capped with AA sites.

Studying the buildings through his zoom lens and noting their proximity to the Detroit River, which linked Lake Erie and Lake Huron, Hunter understood why Roy had shown him that last photo of a warship. If someone *was* looking to throw a sucker punch at RAM, as strange as it sounded, having a warship might not be a bad idea.

He flew on.

About twenty miles southwest of downtown Detroit was a large airport that, in the prewar days, had been called Coleman International. It was now a gigantic RAM air base.

Passing overhead, Hunter saw not just active runways and support buildings blazing with heat signatures, but lots of airplanes also.

The half dozen Mitchells that Roy had told him about were down there, neatly lined up along one of the major runways. But even more alarming, he spotted at least a dozen squadrons of heavy bombers. B-52s, B-58s, and even a few B-47s. There were fifty-four of them in all, a gigantic air fleet these days. Just as bad, he could see hundreds of aerial bombs stacked along the runways, right out in the open.

The RAM was not known for air power. That's why they hired the 10th Street Crew to do their bombing for them.

There was only one explanation for the buildup: The Red Army Mafia was gathering all these heavy bombers for a retaliatory strike on Football City.

And it would not be some dumb-bomb drop on the city's harbor either. With all those big airplanes, such a bombing raid would be like the RAF over Dresden. The aim would be to destroy the city and everyone in it.

And it was all his fault.

Shooting down the dozen bombers the night he'd returned might have been a heroic act that had rejuvenated Football City, but now Hunter was sure it had led to this. . . .

And studying how the heavy bombers were dispersed below him, he guessed they'd be ready to attack in less than seventy-two hours.

Hunter brought the B-57 in for a landing in Football City just before midnight.

He taxied to its hardstand where Ben and JT were waiting. They secured an access ladder and Hunter climbed down. He had the recon camera's videocassette with him.

He told them bluntly, "You're not going to like what you're going to see."

They went to the pilots' mess and had soggy pancakes and cold coffee. They watched the videotape, and JT and Ben saw what Hunter had seen: the firm RAM grip on Detroit and the airfield full of heavy bombers. Football City had faced similar threats in the past, but nothing on this scale.

The question now was: What could they do about it?

After a couple hours of discussion, one thing was clear:

Hunter needed an especially audacious plan if he wanted to preempt RAM's pending carpet bombing of Football City.

At the end of the session, Ben asked Hunter, "So, what do we do first?"

Hunter drained the last of his cold coffee.

"Let's go get a warship."

CHAPTER 11

DEPENDING ON ONE'S POINT OF VIEW, Kingsburg was either the worst part of outer Football City or the best. At one time it was famous for building boats of all sizes; these days, it was a collection of bar rooms, gambling halls, whorehouses, and gun shops. It was not a place for the faint of heart.

Following Roy's instructions, Hunter, Ben, and JT walked into the town's most notorious bar, the Broken Bottle. It was smoky, smelly, and crowded with drunks and hookers.

At one table, seven men were playing cards. Hunter knew they were sailors right away. Their clothes, their mannerisms, their ruddy complexions.

Just the guys they were looking for.

Hunter, Ben, and JT, once again wearing hoodies, boldly pulled up three seats and joined the table uninvited. This startled the sailors. Each pulled back his jacket to show some kind of pistol tucked inside. But Hunter knew how to play the game. He lifted his hoodie to reveal a massive .357 handgun stuck in his belt; Ben and JT did the same. If it was a question of firepower, they'd just won.

Then Ben said the magic words: "Roy sent us."

One of the sailors was older and had a ruddier complexion than the rest. He was an ex-chief petty officer and the group's alpha dog.

"What can we do for you?" he asked gruffly.

"Do you guys own a warship?" JT replied.

"That depends on who's asking," the CPO said.

Ben smiled. "You guys remember Hawk Hunter?"

The men nodded solemnly.

"Ever meet him face-to-face?" Ben asked.

They all shook their heads no.

JT put his hand on Hunter's shoulder. "Well, here's your chance . . . "

Hunter pulled his hood back slightly, so they could get a better look at his face. The sailors' jaws dropped simultaneously.

"You're him?" one man said with a gasp.

"I'm him," Hunter replied.

The men immediately dropped the attitude.

"We heard you came back—some kind of miracle or something," the CPO said. "But I didn't believe it until now. Where the hell have you been?"

Hunter held up his hand and said, "That's top secret, okay?"

Again the sailors nodded soberly.

"So, you need a tin can?" the CPO asked.

"We might," Hunter said. "Can you give us a little background first?"

The men ordered a round of drinks and began their story.

They had been lifers in the US Navy before the Big War. In its aftermath, when America became fractured, they were able to spirit a small destroyer away from the Navy's Great Lakes training school and bring it to Kingsburg. The sailors intended to return it to combat condition, then sell it.

Then one day while on a trip to Football City, the men bet on the city's year-round, nonstop football game and won an enormous payday. Each man's split had been more than five million dollars in gold.

After that windfall, the sailors decided to take a break from restoring the old warship—and that break had lasted more than ten years.

"Having money is not a bad thing," the CPO concluded. "But nothing's like being out at sea."

"So is your ship available to rent?" Hunter asked. "We'll pay you a fair price."

The seven men didn't even discuss it.

"Sorry, you can't rent it," the CPO said, then added, "but you can use it for free."

Hunter was puzzled.

"Free?" Hunter asked. "Why?"

"Because of all you did for our country years ago," the CPO told him. "We just don't forget things like that—so there's just no way we could charge you. But, there is one condition."

"What's that?" Hunter asked.

The CPO smiled and replied, "We go where she goes."

Hunter disappeared the next day.

He was packed and gone before sunrise, long before the crowd had gathered in front of his building, hoping to catch a glimpse of him.

One of Football City's Hueys was gone, too. This left the city with just two eggbeaters, a handful of Sabre jets, and six very old C-119 "Flying Boxcars" as its only airworthy combat aircraft. After being converted to a recon plane, the B-57 no longer qualified.

Hunter had left instructions for Ben and JT before he vanished. An entire notebook of them. It also held a list of items Football City would need if his plan was to be successful. The list included hundreds of parachute flares, a homemade radio jamming pod, nearly a ton of cut-up aluminum foil strips, five large loudspeakers (complete with two-hour-long audio cassettes), and a large shipment of plain, brown boxes mysteriously stamped KEEP AWAY FROM OPEN FLAME in Chinese that Hunter had ordered and that had arrived later that day.

Ben and JT were the keepers of that bible now. They knew that if they followed every step Hunter had laid out, there was a chance, though slim, that the next forty-eight hours might not end in disaster.

But they had a lot of work to do.

CHAPTER 12

THE CITY OF DETROIT had a strict curfew, per the decree of the Red Army Mafia.

It lasted from dusk to dawn, and any civilian caught in the streets during that time was executed on the spot by patrolling RAM security troops.

A total blackout was also imposed across the city—and the punishment for breaking it was just as harsh. Anyone caught with a light on—or even a lit candle—would be hauled into the street and shot.

This was how RAM maintained control of the city. The great mass of its subjects detested RAM, but they were also wise enough not to break the rules.

It was one of the RAM hit squads patrolling the southern edge of the city's limits in an old troop truck that first saw the strange collection of aircraft approaching.

It was odd. RAM aircraft rarely flew in large groups, and almost never at night.

So, whose planes were these?

There was one jet fighter, followed by a half dozen large prop-driven airplanes. Suddenly the formation was over their heads. Those RAM troopers equipped with night-vision scopes could see the backs of the prop planes open up and something tumbling out.

They were boxes . . . plain, ordinary-looking boxes.

But then the boxes began exploding in midair, causing enormous *booms!* Suddenly the sky was filled with thousands of small, individual explosions going off.

Only then did the RAM troopers realize the city was being bombed.

Their radioman tried calling higher authority—but then a second, trailing Sabre jet arrived over the Mackinac Bridge. Its pilot pressed his weapons trigger once, and the RAM patrol was vaporized, truck and all.

With this strange beginning, the Battle of Detroit was underway.

Within minutes, the "boom boxes" were going off all over the Motor City.

The commotion was loud enough that some of the citizens, locked inside their blacked-out homes, dared to look out their windows.

They saw the sky was lit in all directions like daytime. Some of the illumination was coming from flares, dropping slowly on special parachutes designed to hover in the air for long periods of time. But there were also thousands of small blasts going off everywhere. Like millions of strobe lights blinking at once.

The noise was frightening. A loud, earsplitting roar, punctuated every few seconds by the sound of a huge explosion going off. In some parts the city, the noise was so loud, buildings started to crumble.

All this had the RAM security troops patrolling the streets in a major panic. Every last man sought cover to avoid being killed in the bombastic aerial display.

A similar kind of panic ran through RAM headquarters. Lit by the thousands of flashes of blinding light, the seven former-GM towers shook wildly from the noise. Still, their roofs were thick with AA guns and SAM missiles, and some of the RAM crews had started firing back.

But their SAMs were heat seekers, and anything they fired was distracted by the hundreds of red-hot, burning flares drifting over the city. And while their AA guns were radar guided, strips of aluminum foil were also falling out of the prop planes, and as every AA gunner knew, aluminum strips appear on radar screens like massive swarms of bees, masking anything that a radar-guided AA gun might lock on to.

In other words, RAM's anti-aircraft forces had been rendered useless.

RAM had a large and brutal security force, but they were trained for intimidation—not combat. And never had RAM considered that any other city would attack them. But that's what seemed to be happening now—and its top officers had no idea what to do. So they scampered down into their basement shelters and waited as the city they'd controlled for so long was bombed into dust.

Or at least that's what they *thought* was happening.

All communications in Detroit were cut within the opening minutes of the unusual attack.

One of the prop planes circling the city was equipped with Hunter's primitive-but-effective radio jammer, making communication all but impossible. Which is why the officers hiding in the RAM HQ's basement shelters were not getting any damage reports. The noise was deafening, the light was blinding—but what exactly was being destroyed?

There was just no way for them to know . . .

The few RAM officers and AA crews remaining atop the seven towers were still firing away at the mystery aircraft. They could see them flying north, south, and west of the city, still dropping boom boxes, flares, and aluminum strips. Meanwhile, there was no air activity east of the city, along the riverfront, which was why the RAM forces that were still topside had their eyes glued only in the other three directions.

Which turned out to be a big mistake.

The destroyer had slipped into the Detroit River late that afternoon, after a two-day, breakneck journey across two of the Great Lakes. It had been lurking a few miles to the north since then, moving only when the first bright flashes began going off over the Motor City.

It sped down the river, stopping when it reached a position parallel to the towers of RAM's headquarters nearby.

Those few security troops guarding the riverfront saw the ship, but mistakenly thought it belonged to RAM. Suddenly a helicopter came out of the night and roared right over them. They knew RAM had no helicopters, but this one was flying so quickly, they couldn't even see it, never mind fire on it.

Nor did they see the three big guns on the ship's deck turning toward the seven towers of RAM headquarters.

Hunter flew the helicopter with ease.

Handling the chopper had just come naturally to him. Even setting down on the extremely small helipad he'd set up on the destroyer's stern had been a breeze.

Climbing to five hundred feet, he saw what the enemy saw— a sky full of blinding aerial pyrotechnics—and he heard what the enemy heard—the sound of gigantic explosions, mostly courtesy of the huge Football City stadium speakers.

It was all very scary, even to him. But that was all part of the plan.

He flew around the seven towers once, neatly dodging those few ordinary antiaircraft guns that had lowered their barrels to shoot at him. He spotted people on the upper floors looking out at him; they were all adult males in uniform. If what he had planned worked, those people were breathing their last breaths.

He opened up an unimpeded radio link to the destroyer and was soon talking to the CPO in charge. Hunter rattled off a series of numbers, including wind speed, distance to target, throw weight, and wind jam—all vital information for an artillery strike.

Then he said the words that every artilleryman worth his salt longed to hear: "Fire for effect . . ."

Seconds later the ship's six three-inch deck guns opened up. The combined fusillade made the destroyer look like a battleship, further lighting up the night. Its fiery shells passed through the smoke and mist, each one smashing into the midsection of Tower One.

The destroyer's gunners had been right on the money. Tower One was instantly aflame from the twentieth floor up.

Then it was on to Tower Two . . .

In all, it took just five minutes. A total of eight barrages from the destroyer—the extra volley for Tower Four, the tallest and central tower of the seven. Hunter was sure it was the main building of RAM's headquarters. It also seemed to be the most reinforced.

So for the eighth and final barrage, he had the ship's guns fire low, through the flaming wreckage of the other towers, impacting perfectly near the base of the center skyscraper. The massive explosion caused the tower to slowly topple over, hitting the burning building to its south and causing it to topple, too. The noise was tremendous.

Five minutes. That's all it took to reduce the seven evil skyscrapers to smoking rubble. Five minutes to destroy the heart of ten years of RAM tyranny.

Hunter called back to the destroyer and gave them the good news. Then he had one last order for them: "Get out of here—fast!"

Hunter spent the next few hours flying above the shocked, smoking city, making sure that any remaining RAM forces he could see were attacked and eliminated.

To that end, he served as a forward air controller, calling

down air strikes and strafing missions for the pair of Football City Sabre jets Ben and JT were flying.

When they finally had to return home for fuel, Hunter used the Huey's two 50-millimeter cannons to tear up any sign of RAM activity he could find.

Tanks, trucks, gun emplacements.

If he saw it, it was little more than smoke and twisted metal seconds later.

The sky was just becoming light when the helicopter's low-fuel light finally snapped on.

Hunter steered toward Coleman Airport. Ben and JT had refueled and returned to Detroit by that time, landing just as Hunter arrived.

The six C-119s had also refueled and returned; they were carrying more than fifty reserve pilots now in the employ of Football City. The air jockeys were crucial to the next part of the mission.

Hunter landed and met up with Ben and JT. They quietly congratulated each other on the—mostly—psyops mission they'd just pulled off.

No aerial bombs? Not needed, if you have tons of fireworks, smoke bombs, flares, and loudspeakers blaring the sound of explosions at decibel levels that could literally cause one's ears to bleed. Besides, the only real destruction was to RAM's head-quarters and its military apparatus. The city was still standing.

Only the devils were gone.

But with the light of day, all that seemed like a distant mem-ory. Now something new was happening.

St. Louis had arrived with a group of Football City's top military people. With Hunter, Ben, and JT in tow, they walked to the center runway, where they were met by a like number of the people from Detroit's small-but-resilient anti-RAM insur-gency, known as the Motor City Underground (MCU).

In an agreement hammered out just hours before the bat-tle, the MCU leader told St. Louis that in exchange for taking down RAM, the vast armada of RAM bombers now belonged to Football City, along with all the aerial bombs they could carry.

This included the Mitchells Roy from Troy had bought, only to lose to RAM thievery.

So the operation had been a success. RAM was history, Detroit was still intact, and once they were able to integrate the big planes into their tiny air corps, Football City would have one of the largest bomber fleets on the continent.

"From worst to first," JT said as the first B-52s were taking off. "Who'll dare screw with us now?"

Yet the whole thing seemed surreal to Hunter.

The foggy airfield, the sound of airplane engines, the smell of exhaust . . .

His memory began to stir again. He recalled the scene on the foggy runway again, only this time it took place at night. And again came the blur of something moving at an earsplitting speed overhead. Then the mystery woman with blonde hair appeared, beckoning to him through the mist.

Or was she waving goodbye?

He didn't know.

Because, try as he might, he couldn't recall anything more than that.

PART FOUR

THE MAN
NOT ZHANG

CHAPTER 13

One week later

THE SIX MITCHELLS CAME OUT of the night and roared over Groom Lake.

Led by Hunter's F-86 Sabre, they were flying just fifty feet off the ground, engines making a lot of noise, ready to fire at anything that moved.

But the only thing moving at Area 51 was the wind.

It was midnight and the end of a long flight from Football City. Three of the Mitchells were crammed with fifteen people each: two pilots and a flight engineer, plus a dozen members of the Football City Special Forces. The FCSF soldiers took turns manning each plane's gun turrets, but there was no need. The flight out had been unopposed and, after four provocative passes, no one was shooting at them from the secret base below.

But while it seemed like nothing had changed since his recon just ten days before, Hunter still wanted to be the first to land. If a bullet was out there waiting for someone, he wanted it to hit him.

So he brought the Sabre down and rolled it off the runway.

Killing the engine, he lifted his canopy, climbed out onto the wing, and waited.

Nothing.

He jumped to the ground, stopped, and listened.

Still nothing.

He took a moment to absorb his surroundings. It was odd being out here in a place that had fueled so many wild imaginations.

UFOs. Aliens. Bigfoot. Elvis . . .

Where did the truth end and the nonsense begin?

At the same time, his psyche was ablaze. There were answers for him out here . He could feel it. But how quickly could he find them?

He scanned the base with his night-vision goggles. Lots of hangars, support buildings, and old barracks-like structures all appeared empty and abandoned. Just what he wanted to see.

His idea was to get the raiding force on the ground, find Dr. Pott's AII facility, take whatever they could from it, then leave as quickly as possible.

With luck, they'd be there less than an hour.

The B-25s came in one by one.

The first was carrying an FCSF combined air defense and communications team, armed with both Stinger missiles and powerful radio sets able to listen in on AMC radio traffic.

The next three Mitchells were carrying elite FCSF infiltration troops (the raid's search teams). Next to land was the gas plane, filled with huge rubber bladders full of aviation fuel. Its crew would immediately gas up the other Mitchells, readying them for their planned quick exit.

Ben and JT were the last to land. Along with a dozen FCSF troopers, they were carrying two extra passengers: Dr. Pott, who would help look for the AII facility, and St. Louis, who couldn't be talked out of joining the mission.

As a few FCSF troopers took up guarding the Mitchells, the

rest began a building-by-building search, looking for the AII facility, but also making sure there was no opposition hidden anywhere.

Meanwhile, Dr. Pott and St. Louis joined Ben and JT at Hunter's position.

"Anything look familiar, Doctor?" Hunter asked.

"I'm not sure," Pott replied, glancing around. "This place has changed a lot since I was last here."

Pott was assigned a trio of FCSF troopers under St. Louis's command. Together, they headed deeper into the base in search of the AII Research Center.

Hunter, Ben, and JT scouted the south end of the base. They searched a trio of large hangars, but each was empty. They checked a series of smaller buildings, workshops, and toolsheds. They were also vacant, with many broken windows and unlocked doors. The same went for a row of maintenance garages.

"Talk about a ghost town," JT remarked. "I don't blame anyone for not coming out here."

Suddenly Hunter's radio crackled to life. They'd been on the ground less than five minutes.

It was St. Louis.

He said three words: "We found it!"

They'd located the Anomalous Incident Investigation facility inside a large, wooden building squeezed between two enormous, empty hangars built after Pott had left the program.

St. Louis met Hunter, Ben, and JT at the door. "Fried brain or not," he said, "the good doctor led us right to it."

They walked into the dark building to find it filled with dusty computers, moldy furniture, and more broken glass. Pott was waiting by a door at the far end of the hallway. Its sign read: AII SPECIAL RESEARCH STORAGE SECTION.

He was smiling broadly. "Welcome to the end of the rainbow."

They entered a cavernous storage room with boxes stacked

to the ceiling. Small, airtight glass cases lined its walls; other larger containers were located nearby.

Pott explained the glass cases contained items AII had been studying before the program finally closed down.

"Prepare yourselves," he said. "This is pretty strange . . . "

He directed his flashlight on the first case. Inside was an object that looked like an ordinary football, yet was white and stitched like a baseball.

"That's how they play some sport, somewhere else," Pott said.

He pointed his flashlight at the second glass case. It held a dusty photo album opened to a page showing New York City in the 1930s, with two Empire State Buildings standing side by side. The photo's caption read: EMPIRE STATE TWIN TOWERS.

The third glass case held three liquor bottles. One was a bottle of beer, and on its label was printed: SERVE WARM. The second was a bottle of champagne. Its label advised: SHAKE WELL BEFORE USING. The third was a bottle of sake. Its label read: ICE MAKES IT NICE.

All of the items looked normal but different at the same time.

"How did all this stuff get here?" JT asked.

Pott said, "I guess my colleagues must have found a way to retrieve these items from 'somewhere else.' Other places. Other universes."

"But how?" Hunter asked, astonished by the bizarre artifacts.

Pott just shrugged. "I don't know."

At that moment, a trio of FCSF troopers hurried past. They were carrying computer drives, external storage devices, and boxes of written files—data-rich items found inside the storage room. They were taking everything out to the Mitchells.

"Once I get into that stuff," Pott told Hunter, "I'll be able to tell you more."

Standing in the middle of the chamber was the biggest display of all. Even in the shadows they could see it was at least sixty feet long and maybe forty feet wide.

It was covered with metal sheathing wrapped in chains that were locked tight. A couple of FCSF troopers were trying to undo the locks.

"We have no idea what's inside there," Pott said. "But like everything else, we'll find out soon."

St. Louis put his hand on Hunter's shoulder. "It's the treasure trove we were hoping for, Hawk," he said. "I'm sure with all this data, we'll find out what happened to you—and a whole lot more."

Hunter almost choked up. He hadn't expected the moment to be so emotional, but it was. His psyche felt like it was on fire now—things he just *had* to know were finally within his grasp.

He turned to thank Pott, when suddenly . . .

Gunfire.

Then people shouting.

Then more gunfire.

All of it coming from a hangar nearby.

Hunter groaned as he, Ben, and JT rushed out the door.

"I knew it couldn't be *this* easy . . . " JT said.

CHAPTER 14

THE GUN BATTLE WAS OVER by the time they arrived.

A squad of FCSF troopers was standing around five bodies lying in front of a medium-size hangar. The bodies were clothed in black, with weapons that looked like sci-fi movie props. Futuristic helmets hid their faces.

JT gasped. "Jesus—are they ETs?"

Hunter sought out the FCSF squad leader whose unit had been involved in the brief firefight.

"We were securing the next hangar over," he explained. "We came upon these guys trying to drag someone out of this building. They fired at us. So . . . "

Hunter studied the hangar in question.

"Someone's inside there?" he asked.

The squad leader nodded. "Ready for this?"

He opened the door to reveal the hangar was filled with people. Men, women, teens, the elderly—dirty, ragged, and hollow-eyed. In the green tint of night vision, they looked like ghosts, hundreds of them. They were hugging the FCSF troopers as if they'd just been liberated from a concentration camp.

"What is this?" Ben exclaimed. "A homeless shelter?"

The squad leader shrugged. "It's the only locked building we came to. Windows, all the doors, sealed tight from the outside."

A middle-aged man wearing an old army jacket was brought forward. The squad leader said to him, "Tell these guys what you told me."

The man's eyes were wide with fear.

"We're all street people," he began shakily. "There're lots of us these days. We were abducted down in Santa Monica a week ago. We were probed, and then locked up here."

Hunter was incredulous. "By who? Who did this to you?"

"These creatures," the man replied, pointing at the bodies. "They're *eating* us!"

Hunter tried to calm him, but the man was becoming extremely agitated.

"They come out of the ground every few hours," he went on, catching his breath. "And they take some of us—and whoever they take down the Hole, don't come back. I'm telling you they're *eating* us down there!"

"But *who* are *they*?" Hunter asked him again, to which a number of the street people shouted back: "Zombie Aliens!"

"Look at this," the man said, rolling up his ragged sleeve to reveal a tattoo. It read: TEST SUBJECT—WARM TO MAXIMUM POWER.

"I don't know where this came from," he said. "But that sounds like something from a recipe to me. And we all got them!"

Hunter looked at Ben and JT. They were just as bewildered as he was.

Hunter returned to the five bodies. He knelt down beside one, not quite sure what to expect. He slowly lifted the helmet's visor.

What he saw beneath was a heavily scarred face and a pair of dead eyes.

But most important, the body was human—and Asian.

"AMC . . . " he whispered.

The building the AMC soldiers had emerged from was as bland as everything else on the base. Located just across from "Hobo Hangar," it was the size of a two-car garage.

Hunter, Ben, and JT were outside its door, checking their ammo loads. Wearing AMC uniforms, helmets and all, they were going down the Hole to see if what the street people told them was true.

St. Louis was nervous though.

"This really isn't part of the plan," he was saying to Hunter. "I called back home. The C-119s are flying out, and we'll get these poor people out of here. But remember we don't want to start a war with these AMC guys. Not yet anyway."

Hunter understood, but he replied, "What happens to the next bunch of civilians the AMC kidnaps? And what is the AMC doing to them? Those people might be down on their luck, but they're still Americans. We've got to protect them too."

Because of this unexpected twist, Hunter knew they'd have to stay at Area 51 longer than he'd planned.

"I just hope all we find down there is a little clubhouse with a few AMC freaks who are into killing bums."

They entered the empty building and spotted an open door in the far corner. Inside was a small closet, not two feet square. Its floor was missing. Below was a vertical shaft with a ladder that went down one hundred feet to a metal floor. It looked like the entrance to a missile silo.

They switched on their night-vision goggles and down they went. Reaching the bottom, they found themselves in a dark tunnel that went in only one direction. They started walking . . . and walking . . . and walking. Finally, after what seemed like miles, they came to a massive sliding door. It was at least thirty feet in diameter and made of thick steel. It was connected to a huge bank of motors and chains, the mechanism by which the giant door opened and closed.

But at the moment it was slightly ajar.

"They don't lock their front door?" JT asked.

They approached the opening carefully, hoping not to meet any real AMC soldiers coming the other way.

Reaching it, Hunter slowly slid the door all the way open . . . and that's when everything turned fantastic.

There was no other way to describe it.

They found themselves on a gantry, fifty feet long, ten feet wide, with a metal grille railing on one side and the walls of a cavern on the other.

From there, they were looking out on an immense open chamber. It was like the biggest, grandest, most futuristic movie set imaginable. Its walls were thick with glowing white tubes, wire busses, giant fluorescent lights, and fast-moving glass elevators. At least twenty floors below, a huge ground floor contained towering banks of computers, consoles, and control panels displaying hundreds of screens, all generating bright circus-color lights, many of them blinking in unison. It was hypnotic and beautiful in a way. And definitely not military issue.

But the most fantastic thing of all: hanging along one side of the vast chamber were a dozen platforms, almost like a vertical parking lot. Sitting on each platform was what could only be described as a UFO.

Most were the basic flying-saucer design, maybe twenty feet across and colored bright yellow, red, or emerald. Others were shaped like spheres of pure silver. Still others were cigar shaped. In a word, they looked "otherworldly."

Seeing all this, the three of them could barely speak.

Finally JT said, "There were always rumors about underground stuff out here, a place where the military kept UFOs. And we just found it . . . "

"You mean the AMC found it," Ben corrected him.

This was true. The ground floor was crawling with AMC soldiers and white-coated technicians.

The center of their attention was a massive apparatus that looked like a giant ray gun. Small armies of technicians were walking around it, servicing it, checking it, admiring it. Directly in front of it was an immense hole that appeared bottomless.

"Look at the size of that thing," JT said, meaning the giant ray gun. "What the hell does it do?"

Lying flat on the balcony floor and looking through the metal railing, they watched as AMC technicians rolled an old

US Army Hummer to a spot about fifty feet from the ray gun on the other side of the bottomless pit. Once in place, someone pushed a button and a burst of light shot out of the ray gun, hitting the Hummer. An instant later the Hummer was gone.

"Goddamn," Hunter breathed. "Did I just see that?"

Another Hummer was quickly moved into place. It too was hit by a beam and disappeared.

Then a two-ton troop truck was positioned and zapped. It vanished as well.

It was incredible. . . .

But then Ben noticed something. "What are those leftover things?"

After every object vanished, a pile of what looked like glowing embers appeared. They didn't seem to quite touch the floor, though, as if they were hovering just above it. But now, after the three demonstrations, someone hit another button and a series of fans came on and blew the "embers" into the bottomless pit.

"That's either an alien-built weapon," Ben said, "or years ago someone found out how to zap all the hazardous material they were generating out here, so they could get rid of the evidence."

Hunter studied the strange surroundings. He could see only two places in the vast chamber where one could enter or exit. One was another immense open door at ground level. It led out to another astonishing aspect of the chamber: an underground roadway, which they could clearly see from their position. It looked like a four-lane interstate, except it had been built inside a massively hollowed-out cavern. From the scope of it, it had to run for miles.

The only other means of entry was the big, round door they'd just passed through to get on to the gantry. Other than that there were no emergency exits, no other doors, at least none that could be seen.

Some hustle and bustle below indicated the beginning a

shift change. Soldiers and technicians filed out the huge door leading to the underground roadway as an equal number filed in. The relieved shift got into trucks and disappeared down the cavern highway. The new shift went right to work, pampering the immense ray gun.

"Two doors," Hunter said, almost to himself. "That's it."

Then he noticed something else. He pointed to the numerous conical-shaped dishes around the chamber. Most were about one-foot across. They were hanging everywhere, hundreds of them.

Hunter also saw lots of techs on the ground floor using what looked like ordinary handheld phones as controls instead of flicking switches and pushing control buttons.

"I think this place is run by sound waves," he whispered to Ben and JT. "I'm guessing whoever built it didn't want anyone to know they were down here. So instead of using a lot of electrical stuff and generators and creating heat and making noise, they run it all by bouncing sound waves back and forth via those handheld phones. It's like everything is handled by remote control and sound is the transfer medium."

"It would be a good way to lower your power output and reduce your IR signature," Ben whispered back. "Not to mention your noise level. I mean, you can hear a pin drop in here."

It *was* very quiet inside the huge chamber.

Hunter added, "And if each sound transmission is unique, you could have a million different signals running through this place easily."

The shift change complete, the ray gun technicians were getting ready to zap another target.

But it was not a Hummer or a big truck this time.

About twenty ragged people were being led onto the expansive ground floor. They resembled the people they'd found in the hangar except these people were gagged and their wrists were bound. Ten were pulled out of the line and, fighting all the way, were forced into position by AMC soldiers.

Somehow the ray gun was activated, a beam shot out of it—and the people were gone.

Hunter was stunned; Ben and JT, speechless.

Before they could say a word, the remaining ten unfortunates were put in front of the ray gun and dispatched the same way.

Then the fans were turned on and the strange glowing embers left behind were blown into the bottomless pit. It all happened in less than a minute.

"Christ," Ben finally whispered. "I know the AMC hates Americans, but is that what this is all about? Is this . . . "

He couldn't say the words.

So JT said them for him: "Ethnic cleansing?"

They crawled out of the Hole about twenty minutes later.

St. Louis and some FCSF troopers were waiting for them.

Hunter told them everything. The long tunnel. The big door. The fantastic chamber. The UFOs. The underground highway. The ray gun zapping Hummers, trucks, and people.

"It looks like that place has been down there for a while," he said. "I'm guessing the AMC just started using it recently and were careful to make all this up here look unoccupied, so no one would suspect all the action was underground. But whatever's going on, we've got to do something about it."

No one disagreed. But St. Louis said what was on everyone's minds: "But *what* are we going to do exactly? There are only a few dozen of us, and it sounds as if there are hundreds of them down there—and hundreds more right down the road in Vegas. And *thousands* more down in L.A."

Hunter started to say something—but then stopped.

Suddenly his body was vibrating. His eyes turned dark.

"Something is coming. I have to go—right now!"

He started away, but Ben grabbed his arm.

"But Hawk," he said, "if you go, who's going to, you know, come up with a plan?"

JT was very interested in his answer as well.

Hunter paused. He knew Ben and JT were considered the

Wingman's wingmen. But they must have been doing something right to survive during his ten "missing years."

"Who's going to come up with a plan?" he said, throwing their question back at them as he put his helmet on. "I'm sure you guys can handle it."

CHAPTER 15

HUNTER'S SABRE WAS TEARING DOWN Groom Lake's runway a minute later.

The feeling . . .

Something *was* coming . . .

Airplanes . . .

Not friendly . . .

He screamed up to twenty thousand feet and saw them: two jet fighters wearing the triple red-ball symbol of the AMC, cruising at 15-Angels, about five miles away.

These planes weren't old-timers like the Sabre. They were the same high-tech, swept-back, modern aircraft he'd seen during his recon of Nellis, identified off his surveillance footage as J-11s, a fearsome, Chinese-built fighter jet.

And they were heading right toward Area 51.

The jets undoubtedly carried infrared devices, and even if they were just on a night-training mission, if their IF gear was engaged, the pilots would see the activity at Groom Lake. And if they were carrying weapons, they might attack the FCSF force, or at very least report back to Nellis with the news.

Hunter couldn't let that happen.

He watched them for a few seconds, praying they'd turn

away. But they stayed on course to fly right over Area 51. He took a deep gulp of oxygen. He knew tangling with them would blow the lid off the entire operation.

But he had no other choice.

He dove on them, machine guns ablaze. There was no need to aim; no need to even think about it. This was not a dog-fight—it was an assassination. His barrage instantly killed the lead pilot, causing his jet to flip over and clip the one behind him. Both burst into flames and crashed to the desert floor below.

His attack lasted just a few seconds, but everything had changed.

His quick, in-and-out mission was about to get very complicated.

CHAPTER 16

GENERAL ZHANG JIN was the AMC officer in charge of the operation beneath Groom Lake—or at least that's what the AMC personnel working around him thought.

Zhang Jin was not his real name, not that it mattered. He had the reputation of being a harsh commander and failure to obey him carried the death penalty, and that was important. But he wasn't really a "general," or even a soldier at all.

He was in America, all were told, to conduct a "house-cleaning." To rid the American Southwest of Americans, to make room for people from the other side of the Pacific. But even that wasn't entirely true. Before the AMC went ahead with its racial cleansing, they needed to solve the "Nazi Problem," which meant they needed an expert. This man, not Zhang, was that expert. In fact, he might have been the only person on the planet who knew *how* to solve the problem. When he offered the AMC his services right out of the blue, they couldn't hire him quickly enough.

The Nazi Problem posed a dilemma to any entity seeking to eradicate a sizable percentage of humanity. The problem was, when it came to genocide, there were always too many bodies. You couldn't bury them all—it would take years. You couldn't cook them all—the ovens would have to be enormous and expensive, and even then you'd still have to dispose of the leftover ashes, millions of pounds of them a year. And if you were somehow able to drop millions of corpses into the ocean, they would eventually pollute the seven seas.

This man, actually known by many names, had come upon a solution: a machine that could zap things into nothingness, the only residue being some strange little sparks that lasted a long time and could be disposed of by simply blowing them into a bottomless pit. That's what the big ray gun did. Put any object in the right spot, activate its trigger and—poof! Gone . . .

The man knew about the big ray gun because he'd seen it operate years before, when the people who had originally built the chamber, and the road and the cavern beside it, had still been encamped there, experimenting with everything from nuclear bullets to Velcro to jumping universes. He'd seen the big ray gun another time, too, approximately seven thousand years in the future.

But he wasn't sure exactly when, because some of the memories from that part of his very long life were a bit fuzzy.

The cavern below Groom Lake—some called it "S4"—was the perfect place to carry out this mission, and not just because the big ray gun and the bottomless pit were here. S4 lay beneath one of the most isolated places on Earth. It had good terrain cover, no huge energy footprint, and there were few ways to get in or out of it. And it was quiet. Very quiet. And as with submarines and stealth planes, quiet meant invisible. And invisible was ideal. It would take an army of experts to find them down here. It was no surprise that this was where the previous occupants hid all their UFOs.

It also had a highway that ran all the way to Las Vegas *underground*. That came in extremely handy for someone like the Man Not Zhang who was always trying to stay out of sight.

The Man Not Zhang presided over this place from a pod four stories above S4's ground floor.

The pod had darkened windows, so no one could look in. But even if they could, they would not see his face, because he'd decided to wear a mask for this particular outing. He was dressed in all black as usual, head to toe, boots to hat, and the mask was black as well. Two slits for eyes were all he required; he hadn't breathed in anything in centuries, so no nose holes were needed.

When the time came to actually zap some of the great unwashed subjects brought to him from above, the Man Not Zhang rarely activated the big ray gun himself. While its trigger was the most prominent thing on his main console, he couldn't be bothered with the technical end of things. (In fact, he wasn't even sure how the damned thing worked; all he really knew was that activating a button made things disappear.) He had two aides with him around the clock. When it came time to do the dirty work, he would usually just wave his hand in their direction and one of them would push the right buttons on his handheld phone, the phone would make the right noise, and—poof! Gone . . .

They'd been doing it down here for a few weeks now and so far everything was running well. To that end, the masked man had a couple milestones he wanted to reach. His first was to dispatch several hundred test subjects within, say, a twenty minute period, then study the logistics. Bump it up a little, and maybe one thousand an hour wouldn't be unreasonable. It was mostly a matter of getting the unwilling subjects to stand exactly where you wanted them. Figure out that little quirk and expand the already expansive facility, it might be possible to do ten thousand or more an hour or even in one shot.

That was the beauty of the big ray gun. It didn't make any difference how many targets you put in front of it, just as long as they were placed within its "field of vision." Beyond that, the line could stretch to infinity and everybody and everything within it would be gone.

So, make S4 a little bigger, work out the logistics of getting a regular, unending flow of undesirables down into it, and Area 51 could become the AMC's eradication factory, just like that.

It was now close to 0200 hours, 2 a.m.

The masked man looked out on the chamber from his perch. He'd zapped more than two dozen subjects already that night and was expecting another group from up top to arrive soon. (At last report, they were still in the tunnels.) If these people went with no problem, the Man Not Zhang would try a hundred test subjects before the night was out.

But then his radiophone started beeping.

He was soon speaking to the AMC commander at Nellis, seventy-five miles to the south. The man had some startling news: two of his jet fighters on a night-training mission had been shot down very close to Groom Lake. Nellis had no idea who did it or what it meant. But as a result, Nellis was now in a high-emergency security mode.

And with that, the Nellis CO hung up—or his line went dead. It was hard to tell.

Either way, the Man Not Zhang was furious. The AMC was a confederacy of idiots; he'd witnessed a lot in the past few months, but he'd chosen to put up with them, just to see where all this would lead. But the one thing he didn't think they could possibly fuck up was security for S4 and its environs. In the past, this lair had existed with millions of people living within a 250-mile radius. These days, barely twenty-five thousand people lived between there and Los Angeles. And the AMC couldn't even handle that?

But the masked man knew what he had to do. He turned to his aide and held up three fingers. That meant Procedure 3 had to be enacted. But the aide paused for a moment; he wasn't quite sure what Procedure 3 was. The Man Not Zhang punctured the aide's eyeballs with his two long fingernails, casually blinding him. The second aide began enacting Procedure 3 instantly.

S4 was going into lock down. Everyone anywhere inside had to freeze in place until security guards checked their ID badges.

This was the first time the procedure had been enacted inside S4. The roughly three hundred techs and soldiers inside the chamber had to stop working, stop moving, until the security sweep was complete.

Even though everything had suddenly become uncertain, Procedure 3 gave those three hundred people a rare opportunity to at least stand still and not work for a few minutes.

Not able to relax, though, were the thirty people who'd entered the S4 chamber just seconds after the security alert was called.

They were stuck on the top-level gantry. The big round door had slid shut behind them, warning buzzers were going off all round them, and security men with megaphones were shouting up to them from below, telling them to stay in place until they could take an elevator up to them and check their IDs.

This was not good—because five of this group of thirty were FCSF operators in AMC uniforms, Ben and JT among them.

Their plan had been to come back down to the chamber, same as before, in AMC uniforms. But this time, they'd bring a "bladder bomb" filled with aviation fuel with them, drop it on the big ray gun, and destroy it. Then, if possible, eliminate as many of AMC personnel below as possible.

The plan had been bold, simple, and highly workable. It was probably very close to what Hunter would have come up with himself.

It was just their bad luck to get caught inside S4 seconds into its first-ever security lockdown.

CHAPTER 17

THE AIR DEFENSE SYSTEM AT NELLIS was modern for the times, integrating fixed SAM launchers with mobile AA guns into one central control house. But because the base's AMC commanders never dreamed they would be attacked from the air, this powerful-but-expensive ADS was rarely turned on.

But then came the brief-but-chilling radio call from one of Nellis's pilots participating in a night-training exercise. The base went on immediate high alert, with the air defense system finally switched on.

But it was already too late.

The Sabre jet roared over Nellis just seconds after the two J-11s were confirmed as lost. Flying just twenty-five feet off the deck, its first target was the checkerboard-painted air defense control station. A well-placed five-second burst from the plane's machine guns was all it took. The air defense hub burst into flames.

The attacker stayed low. A hard bank to the right, and it sent a barrage into the base's communication building, shredding its main computer and setting the building ablaze.

The silver jet then banked hard left, went up to fifty feet and fired again, destroying the base's control tower and killing most of its personnel. Then another hard right and it was gone, lost in the night.

While not quite sure about what had just happened, the base commanders quickly scrambled Nellis's interceptor unit. Six highly trained veteran pilots were in their J-11 jets inside a minute.

J-11s needed only thirty seconds to warm up and get rolling. Before another minute went by, the six of them were already taxiing for take off.

But they had moved too late as well.

The silver jet roared back over the base, the intense glow of Las Vegas to the east masking its approach. It came down the base's main runway heading south, just as the half dozen J-11s were taking off, heading north.

The jet fired six quick, perfectly timed bursts into each plane, hitting their full gas tanks. All six jets blew up before they got off the ground. The silver jet continued down the length of the runway and fired on the base's external communications antenna, severing its mast, before vanishing into the night again.

With many major fires suddenly erupting, the base's emergency crews were called out—but chaos and panic had already set in. The ghostly jet roared over the huge airfield a third time, just twenty seconds after it had left, and fired a long, sustained burst into the base's enormous and unprotected fuel dump. The tanks blew up so quickly, the attacker had to pass right through the flames it had created.

But then it was gone for good.

Hunter yanked off his oxygen mask and breathed in the hot air of the cockpit.

He'd left Nellis reeling—taking out its scramble jets and its fuel supply; making it electronically blind and deaf; and fouling its main runway.

But this one-man preemptive strike bordered on desperation, and he knew it. It would serve as a holding action at best, because once the AMC figured out all this grief was coming from Groom Lake, they would respond in force.

That's why he *had* to get back there, ASAP.

But then, not thirty seconds outside Nellis, Hunter's body began vibrating again.

Damn . . .

Enemy airplanes.

Still flying at fifty feet, he looked up to see the bare taillights of two more J-11s at ten thousand feet. They were already diving toward him.

Where they'd come from didn't matter, because Hunter had expended the last of his ammunition taking out Nellis's fuel dump.

Now what?

Suddenly he hit his throttles, climbed to five thousand feet, and turned directly toward Groom Lake. Then he punched his radio to life and made a brief call.

The J-11s were on his tail seconds later. They were armed with the powerful PL-10, a long-range, anti-aircraft missile that was very hard to fool. With his guns empty and the two fighters on the offensive, Hunter had no choice but to run.

The first PL-10 came at him a moment later. He began zigzagging violently, feeling the missile getting closer by the second. Then, just as he sensed it was about to hit, he pulled back on the control stick and went completely over the top. The missile could not follow. He watched as, with its internal guidance confused, it plowed into the desert below.

But a second PL-10 was on his butt an instant later. Hunter kicked his throttles to max and this time went straight up. The missile mimicked his maneuver, but then couldn't match Hunter's sudden sharp loop. The missile lost its way, flared out, and crashed.

Hunter completed his loop and wound up just where he wanted to be: a few hundred feet in front of both enemy fighters.

It was a dangerous move, but he had to stay as close as possible to his pursuers so they couldn't fire any more long-range missiles at him. He would have to endure their cannon fire instead—and hope his strategy worked.

About ten miles outside Area 51, both AMC planes opened up on him, their huge shells going by him like streaks of lightning. He began twisting and turning the Sabre so violently, he could feel its fuselage cracking. More cannon fire. More rolling and dodging, maneuvers so extreme, not only was the fuel flow to his engine being disrupted, but his canopy glass was actually splintering as well.

Then, finally, he could see Area 51 on the horizon.

But would his plan work?

About a quarter mile out, he went back down to fifty feet and started spinning the Sabre wildly. That was his signal. He roared over the runway a few seconds later, the two J-11s still glued to his ass. Their pilots undoubtedly saw the B-25s and the unwarranted activity at Area 51, but at the moment, it didn't matter. Only killing the Sabre did.

Hunter knew this and started counting down from five. At zero, he pulled back on the stick and jammed the Sabre's throttles to max again.

The pair of J-11s followed his maneuver—and that's when two streaks of orange flame came out of the hills near the base.

While the two unsuspecting AMC pilots were trying their best to close in for the kill on the Sabre, two heat-seeking missiles hit them dead on.

The J-11s exploded simultaneously and slammed into the desert floor, victims of the well-hidden FCSF Stinger teams.

Just in time, too, as Hunter's F-86 ran out of gas a second later.

CHAPTER 18

Groom Lake

HUNTER GLIDED IN FOR A LANDING. No sooner had he stopped rolling than the Sabre jet was mobbed by the gas plane's crew. They started refueling and rearming it immediately.

An access ladder appeared, but Hunter was surprised to see the squad leader of the Stinger team climbing up the steps.

Hunter congratulated him on some great shooting, but the man was not there for that. Again, the Stinger crew doubled as the FCSF's communications intercept team. And in just the past few minutes, they'd overheard two pieces of very disturbing news.

"An AMC troop convoy is heading our way," the squad leader told Hunter starkly. "They are above ground. They might have been on night maneuvers or who knows what—but they're definitely coming this way as part of the AMC security emergency. They'll be here in about twenty-five minutes—or less."

Hunter's heart went to his feet. But there was more bad news.

"We intercepted another radio message from L.A.," the

squad leader went on. "Three *planeloads* of AMC troops are flying up from L.A. in giant Antonov cargo jets. That will be about
a thousand troops, probably paratroopers. They're mustering
up now; it's about a one-hour flight once they get airborne.
They'll be here at sunrise."

Hunter stared back at him in disbelief. This was getting serious. He checked his watch. It was now almost 0300 hours, less
than ninety minutes before sunrise. He rubbed his tired eyes
and tried to shake the feeling that the whole world was closing
in on him.

So much for well-laid plans.

He finally climbed out of the Sabre, only to find even *more*
bad news waiting for him.

St. Louis was at the bottom of the access ladder. He looked
extremely worried. Hunter had noticed very few FCSF troopers were about and the ones he could see looked grim and on
guard. After seeing the two AMC planes shot down—with
their remains still burning in the desert nearby—everyone was
expecting some kind of response from the AMC. Even St. Louis
was wearing a helmet now.

He got right to the point.

"Ben and JT went back down the Hole," St. Louis told Hunter
urgently. "Along with three of my guys dressed up like AMC. The
plan was to destroy the big ray gun, so they brought a bladder
bomb with them. They were making like they were leading the
next bunch of hobos down there to be zapped. They got in okay,
but then the place went into lockdown. Everyone was told to stay
in place until they were cleared by the security troops.

"Our guys were stuck out on that big gantry you were on
earlier, not that far from the big round door. They stayed in
place and waited for the security troops to come to them, so
they could get off the first shot. But before that happened,
another security team showed up, this time in back of them, and
they saw our guys getting ready to rumble.

"This second team ordered our guys to turn around, and
that's when everyone started shooting. Then the original secu-

rity team from below arrived—and they tried to shoot our guys in the back. So the hobos had to shoot those guys . . . "

"The hobos . . . shot them?" Hunter asked, incredulous.

St. Louis nodded, out of breath now, and said, "Because they're not hobos—they're another two dozen of my guys dressed in the hobos' clothes."

Hunter was shattered. This place that he'd thought held so many of his memories, so many parts of his life, was now turning into hell on Earth.

"So, we've got *thirty* guys trapped inside?" he asked.

St. Louis nodded soberly. "We have intermittent communication with them," he said, holding up his hand radio. "But we'd be crazy to think it isn't a minute-to-minute situation."

Hunter checked the time again. He knew the C-119s would be arriving at sunrise, but that's when the three huge cargo planes full of AMC troops would be arriving as well. Plus, the AMC land convoy was now just minutes away.

His brain went in overdrive. The overland convoy was the most imminent threat—and he already had an idea for that.

But he also had to conjure up something to help his trapped friends.

Then suddenly it came to him.

The speed of sound . . .

"I'll need about thirty minutes," he told St. Louis while signaling all the B-25 crews to meet him on the runway. "Can Ben and JT hang on that long?"

St. Louis just shook his head. "I guess they'll have to."

The road leading from Nellis to Groom Lake started out as an asphalt highway.

Used as a bus route back in the old days for people who lived in Vegas and worked at Area 51 but didn't like to fly, it went straight through the desert for about fifty miles.

Then, twenty miles from Area 51, it went down to a dirt road that ran between two mesas. With sharp curves at either end, the road traveled about a mile through this pass, before it became straight as an arrow again.

The AMC convoy had left Nellis earlier that evening on night maneuvers. After getting the news that first, two AMC fighters had been shot down, and then that Nellis itself had been attacked, their commanders ordered them to Groom Lake to "assess the situation."

The convoy consisted of three dozen trucks, carrying about five hundred troops. They were on the highway just twenty-five miles south of Groom Lake when they received their orders. And at the moment, they were going at full speed toward Area 51.

Only when the road passed between the two mesas did the convoy slow down a little.

But just as the head of the column was approaching the end of the pass, an airplane came out of nowhere. It was an old two-prop attack bomber, flying slow and making lots of noise—a plane that might get shot down by a single rifle bullet hitting it in the right place.

But the plane suddenly dove on the column and unleashed a storm of cannon fire from its nose, hitting not only the first truck, but the giant towering rocks on either side of the pass as well. This created an avalanche, with two large boulders tumbling down, crushing the truck, and immediately blocking the road.

At the same time, one mile away, the end of the column was just entering the mesa pass road. A similar two-prop aircraft suddenly appeared and did the same thing. It fired barrages at the cliffs on both sides of the pass, triggering another landslide and sealing off any means of retreat.

Now every vehicle in the column hit its brakes, and the parade of troop trucks ground to a halt.

That's when the two old two-prop planes were joined overhead by four more, plus the accursed silver jet.

They peeled out of the sky in a very systematic fashion, the six B-25s and the gleaming Sabre, firing nose cannons, machine guns, and rockets. There were also gunners at the side doors of the Mitchells, , firing twin fifties down on the hapless column.

It was like the Road to Basra. There was nowhere the AMC

soldiers could run, nowhere they could hide. Back and forth, amid the tracers, the huge explosions, the sound of the loud propellers fighting their way through all the smoke, and the scream of the Sabre's jet engine, it took less than fifteen minutes for Hunter and the B-25s to destroy the AMC column and just about everyone in it.

But as Hunter flew one way and the Mitchells the other, he knew it wouldn't be that easy again.

CHAPTER 19

THE SURVIVING AMC ANTI-AIRCRAFT UNITS at Nellis were just coming back online when the mysterious silver jet appeared again.

It came in extremely low, just like the time before, flying under the radar net but making a lot of noise.

No sooner had it arrived than the ADS units opened up. Missiles, AA guns, automatic-weapons fire from the hundreds of base personnel who'd been armed after the first devastating attack. Even the personnel fighting the raging fuel dump fire were armed and shooting at the intruder.

The night was lit up like Baghdad, but somehow the jet made it through the firestorm—and then . . . disappeared.

Only a few people at the base saw what actually happened. After passing over the main runway, the jet made a sharp right hand bank and flew directly into the entrance of the underground highway.

And as improbable as it sounded, the jet was now flying *inside* the huge, hollowed-out thoroughfare.

There might be a time, Hunter realized, when he would just run out of ideas and not be able to come up with a great plan when he needed one. The question was: Would he know it ahead of time? Or would he learn that lesson the hard way, through catastrophe—or even mortal failure?

These thoughts were running through his mind as he simultaneously wondered if S4's underground highway had been built arrow straight or with some curves.

He believed it was straight and his reasoning was simple: whoever constructed the massive subterranean roadway wouldn't have needed to build in any curves or dips. This was the desert. The desert was mostly sand. They just had to tunnel under everything. Right? Because, if not, and he came to a curve or a turn, it would be curtains for him.

And he had another problem. He didn't know where the other end of the underground highway was. He was sure he wasn't flying in a closed system. He could tell he was moving against moving air, which would not be the case if the roadway had a dead end at its terminus. Of course, complicating all this deep thinking, he was flying at more than five hundred miles per hour in a relatively confined space.

That's why just a few seconds into his extreme and possibly harebrained scheme, he thought, "I don't think I've done this before."

He radioed St. Louis, amazed that he could get through. His old friend could barely talk after Hunter told him what he was doing. But Hunter asked him only to relay some information to the FCSF people trapped inside S4, gave him his position, and signed off.

It was about seventy-five miles from Nellis to Groom Lake. At his current rate of speed, Hunter knew he could cover that distance in less than ten minutes.

But once there, would his plan work?

Inside S4

The radiophone had barely beeped once before Ben answered it.

Their only link to the outside world, he was astonished the device was still working at all.

St. Louis was on the other end. Ben could just barely hear him over all the static.

"After doing the math, I'm supposed to say to you, 'seven minutes,' " St. Louis was trying to tell him. "Something will happen in about seven minutes. So pass the word."

Ben's ears perked up. He was in a very precarious position and needed all the information he could get.

The FCSF guys—most of them dressed in hobo clothes—had created two firing lines covering their present location, which was about two-thirds down the top gantry of the S4 chamber. The cavern wall had several natural alcoves where the troopers had set up interlocking firing positions. Firing positions were also established along the gantry's four-foot-high metal railing.

These positions were well thought out, and they had held for the past half hour. That's how long Ben, JT, and the others had been trapped here with units of AMC security troops blocking them at either end of the gantry.

A gunfight in any direction would take a lot of lives, and both sides knew it. So it was a stalemate—at least for now.

But Ben had learned earlier from St. Louis that three huge cargo planes were flying AMC reinforcements into Groom Lake. Plus he assumed the AMC would at least move reinforcements up to S4 via the underground highway. When they arrived, the FCSF unit would eventually succumb to the higher numbers. JT was already calling it the "Custer's Last Stand" option.

For these reasons, Ben was very anxious to hear what Hunter had in mind—specifically, what was going to happen in seven minutes.

Trouble was, St. Louis didn't know.

"He just said be prepared in about seven minutes," he replied when Ben pressed him. "And you know Hawk. He's usually on time."

Traveling 550 miles an hour now, Hunter was surprised how well the old Sabre was performing—twisted fuselage, shattered canopy, and all. He'd been able to hold it steady twenty-five feet above the roadway, leaving another twenty-five feet as a buffer between him and the tunnel's ceiling.

Any deviation though, the slightest dip in altitude or a sway to the left or right, and he'd be a sheen of blood and gas on the asphalt of the underground highway. The only good thing about that scenario was: it would be over quick.

One point in his favor, though: the S4 highway was amazingly well lit. It was lined on both sides with large fluorescent lights so bright he wasn't using his night-vision goggles.

And it was perfectly straight, so far. In fact, his only immediate concern was what he was seeing in front of him—which was nothing but the tunnel, going off into infinity. Appropriately enough, he was getting tunnel vision—and it was somewhat hypnotic. He had to rapidly blink his eyes every few seconds just to get himself reoriented.

But then suddenly he saw something ahead of him, something that interfered with his tunnel vision. It was a line of troop trucks, moving deeper into the tunnel, just as he was.

Before he could even think about it, he was over them and could see it was a half-mile-long AMC troop convoy, no doubt heading for the S4 chamber with reinforcements.

Besides scaring the crap out of the convoy's troops, Hunter was just able to fire his machine guns at the last instant, hitting the first few trucks in line. There was a huge secondary explosion as he flashed overhead, flames chasing him while he continued to barrel down the tunnel.

A quick glimpse over his shoulder told him that he'd disabled several trucks, blocking the tunnel in both directions, at least temporarily.

He let out a breath of relief—only by good fortune had he delayed the AMC from getting more troops to the chamber and tipping the scales their way.

But was he really going to be able to help the FCSF unit trapped inside?

He looked at his watch.

One minute to go . . .

He pushed the throttles all the way forward—and held on tight.

He'd have his answer soon enough.

The first indication JT had that something was happening was when his knees started to shake.

True, he was in a sticky situation, trapped on the upper level of the huge chamber, with bad guys blocking any route of escape. But he'd been in tight spots before, and his knees never shook.

But they were shaking now.

He turned to Ben, who was holding a position looking down the gantry at the AMC nest just thirty feet away, and said, "Can you feel that?"

Ben thought for a moment, then said, "Is everything shaking?"

JT began to reply . . . but the words never came out.

The mild vibration suddenly became a rumbling so loud, so powerful, that the massive S4 chamber started moving—*physically* moving. The gantry began swinging like an amusement park ride, knocking some of the FCSF troopers off their feet.

And then came a gigantic *boom!*

In that instant, no one could talk, no one could hear, no one could even think about anything but the overwhelming, ear-splitting bang—the result of Hunter's jet rocketing past the huge open door leading into the S4 cavern, breaking the sound barrier at the exact right moment.

Everything in the fantastic chamber went dead. All the colors, all the lights, all the means of communication—all of it just blinked out. This place had run on sound waves to keep it hidden all these years. Creating a sonic boom in such a space was like dropping an A-bomb on it. Thousands of circuits were blown out. Other things exploded just from the massive increase in pressure. Many AMC soldiers and techs on the bottom floor suffered from burst craniums, their screams could be heard even over the titanic roar.

It was the moment the FCSF team had been waiting for.

Ben shouted as loud as he could, "Let's go!"

Immediately, JT and half the FCSF troopers attacked the AMC soldiers blocking their way out of the underground chamber. Many of the enemy gunmen were on the floor, writhing in pain from the sudden unexpected sonic blast. Though outnumbered, the FCSF troopers quickly overran them in a brief, one-sided firefight, disabled the controls of the big round door, and opened it manually.

Meanwhile, Ben and the other dozen troopers ran forward, guns blazing. Seeing them charge, the frightened and injured AMC soldiers at the far end of the gantry quickly retreated. This allowed the FCSF squad to light and drop the 50-gallon bladder bomb directly over the ray gun.

They didn't wait for it to explode.

Once they had lifted it over the railing and let it go, Ben just yelled, "Let's get the hell out of here!"

It was only a matter of luck that the Man Not Zhang survived the bladder bomb explosion.

He'd been at the back of his pod about a minute before, monitoring the security situation across an array of fifty-year-old TV screens. Intruders were inside the walls. They'd slipped in disguised as the lowly AMC privates whose only job was to lead lambs to the slaughter—and those dimwits couldn't even do that right.

But Procedure 3 had worked. The intruders, identities unknown, were trapped by his forces on the upper level.

Nellis had promised that an underground convoy of reinforcements would arrive at S4 at any time. The numbers would be overwhelming—and the Man Not Zhang had planned to throw waves of AMC soldiers at the intruders until they ran out of ammunition and were eliminated.

He'd been checking the time, anxious for the AMC reinforcements to arrive, when he heard the most horrendous noise. In the next instant, the sonic boom went through S4 with such concussive power, it penetrated his all-black ensemble and ripped some of the skin from his ancient bones.

Then everything went dark—and the place that for years had been so quiet suddenly had sound waves bouncing off its walls with such violence the walls were crumbling. Machines and lights were shorting out, causing jagged streaks of sparks to spit from every corner of the place. It was like a thunder and lightning storm—contained inside the cavern.

Uncharacteristically staggered, the Man Not Zhang pushed a handheld phone button all by himself, sending a sound wave signal to close the massive door leading from S4 to the underground highway. For some reason he thought that would stop the earsplitting noise.

In the next instant, though, he realized what a foolish thing he'd done—and tried to override the signal. But it was too late. With their last ounces of stored power, those huge soundproofed motors zipped to life, closed the huge door, and then went dead for good.

The masked man began pushing many phone buttons— while screaming orders to his aides to do something, *anything*, before realizing one was blind and cowering in the corner and the other had left long ago—but nothing was working.

Well, not quite nothing . . .

At that moment, the man was treated to an incredible sight: the twelve UFOs that had been sitting above the chamber gathering dust since the AMC had come to this place, suddenly started moving. Like robots, they became airborne all at the same time. Then, incredibly, a hidden door in the chamber— this one on the ceiling—cranked open under its own power, and the UFOs began flying out.

"Cowards . . . " he mumbled through his tattered black mask as the last of the UFOs disappeared.

The bladder bomb hit a second later.

From his point of view, it came out of nowhere—a black, rubbery object falling from the ceiling, trailing a long, thin streak of flame behind it.

It hit the big ray gun dead on and, in that first instant, splattered a great amount of liquid all over the device, its controls—all over everything.

But in the next instant, the liquid exploded and the floor of the S4 chamber was suddenly awash in a tsunami of flames. It blew up with such violence, those flames actually climbed four stories and engulfed the masked man's protruding pod.

He could easily see through flames, though, and what he saw was the ray gun reduced to a mass of smoldering metal, surrounded by the bodies of his now-immolated tech crew.

That was it for him. The end of this housecleaning experiment. What he needed was another great escape, a way to get out of the place before it became his tomb.

He had one last trick, though: When he'd first come to the cavern, the AMC had given him a large box that they said should only be opened in cases like this. Leftover from the original builders of S4, it was to be used only when it appeared that some kind of catastrophic failure had occurred inside the chamber and there was no other way to escape.

He opened this last-ditch box to see, to his astonishment, that it contained . . . a parachute.

"In this place?" he thought.

There were brief instructions. He read them hastily and thought they were pure insanity. But then he read them again—and thought, well, maybe not.

Besides, he had no other choice.

So he strapped on the parachute, and then left his pod, stumbling into the smoke and chaos outside.

He gained his bearings and, picking his way through the debris and the bodies, started for the floor of the chamber below.

Once the big round door was opened and secured, JT and his FCSF troopers set up another defensive firing line to cover to

Ben and the others who'd run ahead to drop the bladder bomb on the chamber floor below.

It was from this position that JT and his group saw the stunning sight of the up-until-then somnambulant UFOs suddenly coming to life and flying out of S4.

JT couldn't believe it. "I knew those things were real!" he shouted above the din.

There were only scattered gunshots chasing Ben and his men as they ran to safety. They too had seen the exodus of the UFOs—just one more crazy thing happening around them.

But then, just a few feet from reaching the new FCSF positions, Ben skidded to a stop.

"Hey!" he yelled to JT. "Look at that . . . "

JT saw Ben pointing down into the chamber. It was lit only by the fires leftover from the bladder bomb, but in the world of night vision, it was like looking into Hell.

Incredibly, they saw a sight even stranger than the fleeing UFOs. On the chamber floor there was a figure clad in black and wearing, of all things . . . a parachute.

Suddenly, the person jumped into the bottomless pit, pulling the ripcord as he did so. He disappeared in a flash.

"What the fuck is *that* about?" JT asked, astonished.

Ben didn't have a clue—it was just too bizarre.

JT yelled to him to get going again. A horde of AMC soldiers was coming their way, knowing the big round door was the only way out of the burning chamber.

"Let's get this door closed," JT said as Ben finally reached the firing line. "We can figure out all this weird shit later."

The entire FCSF team began pushing on the big round door, hoping to slide it shut. They were about halfway into this when the throng of AMC soldiers reached the top of the gantry and began scrambling toward the portal. None of them was firing a weapon; it was beyond that now. They just wanted to get out before the chamber collapsed on itself.

But they were out of luck.

The FCSF troopers plus Ben and JT just managed to close

the door and lock it manually from the other side before the first AMC gunmen arrived.

They could hear the enemy fighters pleading with them to reopen the door, to save their lives, but that just wasn't in the cards.

Once safe on the other side, the FCSF team made sure everyone was accounted for—and then hurried back up top.

CHAPTER 20

WHEN HUNTER FINALLY EXITED the far end of the under-ground highway, just ninety seconds after creating the sonic boom inside S4, he found himself on the other side of Bald Mountain, about twenty miles north of Groom Lake.

The highway's egress point was in an extremely desolate area, just two large recessed holes in the side of the mountain and featuring nothing more elaborate than a truck turnaround.

Even getting out had been an adventure. He exited the underground highway practically going sideways, more expelled from the cavern than flying out of it.

He hadn't anticipated the violent back-blast that resulted from dropping the sonic A-bomb on S4. Its concussion slammed into him just seconds after the boom hit, nearly causing him to spin out of control while still inside the tunnel.

That's why he couldn't get out soon enough. The moment he saw the stars blazing overhead, he pulled back on the stick and went straight up, free once more.

That was something he never wanted to do again.

He went up to five thousand feet and leveled off. All this time he'd been praying that his plan had worked—that his sonic boom had massively disrupted the innards of the S4 chamber. But what happened to the FCSF team within?

Once over Bald Mountain, he could see Area 51 in the distance. He immediately steered toward it. Smoke was coming out of the sides of the mountain, signs the S4 chamber was indeed in the process of being destroyed. All he wanted to do now was land and make sure his friends were okay.

But then, suddenly . . .

His body started vibrating.

The feeling . . .

Something was up here with him.

But what?

Then, up ahead . . . flashes of light.

Different colors. Red, yellow, emerald.

They didn't look like explosions. They looked more like fireworks.

But, this wasn't Detroit. Who would be setting off fireworks way out here?

It took him a few moments to figure out what was happening. Then it hit him. The flight path between him and Groom Lake was filled with . . . UFOs.

Twelve of them.

They were spinning and twirling, climbing and diving, engaging in all kinds of fantastic maneuvers.

Hunter knew these were the same objects he'd seen earlier inside the chamber; somehow they'd gotten out of S4 before the shit really hit the fan. But now he wondered: Were these really UFOs? Or were they something else?

They were soon zooming back and forth right off his nose, almost intimidating in their manner. At the same time, though, they never strayed from blocking his path to Groom Lake.

Almost as if they were . . . guarding Area 51.

That's when he thought maybe these "UFOs" weren't UFOs at all.

Because he didn't get "the feeling" for anything other than aircraft.

Earth-built aircraft . . .

At least that's how he thought it worked.

He put his theory to the test. He fired a few machine gun bursts at one of the objects, intentionally shooting high. As soon as the rounds went over it, the object moved so quickly, Hunter knew no human could possibly be piloting it. Yet he knew they were very "earthly."

In fact, they were acting more like robots.

So when the next one came frightfully close to him, he lined it up and put a burst of .50-caliber rounds right into it.

The bright light emanating from the object suddenly blinked out—revealing an impressive, if slightly outdated UAV inside. A drone electronically dressed up to look like a UFO.

He'd been right. They were little more than aerial robots.

It made sense to him now. This was undoubtedly a ruse that the original builders of S4 had come up with to keep prying eyes away—or, better put, to keep them distracted. Whenever anyone unauthorized got too close to the place, just send up a fleet of flying things that looked like UFOs, and Area 51's reputation as a repository for ETs would be furthered—and everything else done there, and other places close by, quickly forgotten.

It was a brilliant tactic of deflection simply because, UFOs were a lot sexier than whatever else someone suspected was being done at Area 51.

After Hunter shot at a couple more of the UAVs, the remaining drones disappeared into the night, destination unknown.

Finally, he turned toward Groom Lake.

He didn't dare risk a radio call at this point—not with AMC forces so close by. He'd have to land to find out if—

Suddenly, his cockpit was bathed in bright-yellow light. His body froze. At first he thought another wave of memories was about to overcome him.

But it was something stranger than that.

ATTACK ON AREA 51

He looked up and saw an enormous, saucer-shaped craft right above him. Where the hell had it come from? It bore no resemblance to the drones he'd just encountered. It was the size of a battleship and had *hundreds* of blinking lights all over it. And it didn't look like a Hollywood version of a UFO.

It really looked out of this world.

It wasn't dancing around or bobbing and weaving. The saucer-shaped craft had matched his speed perfectly and was flying in formation with him, making no secret that it was watching him.

Then, after just a few moments, as he continued staring at it dumbfounded, the gigantic vessel started vibrating—and then it was gone, disappearing straight up in a flash, moving in a way that defied all laws of aerodynamics.

Hunter was thunderstruck.

He'd never see anything like that.

Or, at least, he didn't think so.

CHAPTER 21

HUNTER COULD SEE THE FIRST FAINT RAYS of dawn lighting up the sky as he set down at Groom Lake.

He was greatly relieved when an access ladder appeared out of the murk and JT came clanging up to the top.

His friend was grinning.

"Don't you know Sabres can't go supersonic in this universe?" JT asked him.

Hunter just patted the top of the F-86's cockpit panel.

"Well, this one does," he replied.

He climbed out of the Sabre and saw frantic activity all over the base.

The several hundred homeless abductees were being helped out of Hobo Hangar by FCSF troops and led onto the main runway.

In the distance, the first of the C-119s could be seen lining up for a landing. The five other Flying Boxcars were right behind it.

Hunter could also see smoke pouring out of many different places around the base itself. From below buildings, out of sewer openings, out of cracks in the nearby mountain. All indications that the massive fire was still raging below.

Ben was waiting at the bottom of the ladder. He gave Hunter a bear hug, and so did JT.

"Once I get my hearing back," Ben joked, "remind me to buy you a drink."

"I'll buy you two," Hunter replied, adding, "By the way, did you guys see anything funny flying overhead in the last few minutes?"

They both laughed. "Something funny? Flying around here?" JT replied incredulous. "You've got to be kidding. . . . "

At that moment, St. Louis appeared. He too embraced Hunter and then gave him an update.

"The Stinger guys say the three AMC cargo planes are just twenty-five minutes away. And we can be sure that the AMC will be sending another convoy up from Nellis, too. Now we're all still in agreement we don't want to start a war with these guys now—right?"

Hunter nodded emphatically. Ben and JT did too.

"Time to bug out," JT said anxiously.

But then Hunter asked St. Louis, "Do you have enough stuff from the AII to make the trip worthwhile?"

"More than enough," St. Louis assured him. "But there's something in that storage room that you've still got to see."

Hunter was surprised.

The first C-119 had landed and the first group of homeless was being loaded in. The other C-119s were coming in as well. The area could be engulfed by AMC troops at any moment, plus a huge fire was burning below.

So why did St. Louis want him to go with him?

St. Louis anticipated the question.

"Trust me," was all he said.

He led Hunter back to AII storage room.

It was practically empty. All of AII's data had been recovered, including all of the strange artifacts, and put aboard the Mitchells.

But it was the big glass case in the middle of the chamber

that immediately caught Hunter's eye. It had been covered over last time he saw it.

Now the covering was gone.

Hunter took one look at what was inside the case and felt his whole body go numb.

"God . . . " he breathed. "Am I dreaming this?"

St. Louis smiled, and said, "If you are, then we all are."

Inside the huge case was a jet airplane. It was long and sleek, and its delta-configured wing started up near the cockpit and went all the way to the tail.

It was painted red, white, and blue, and looked absolutely fierce, as if it were going many times the speed of sound even though it was standing still.

"Is that my plane?" Hunter whispered, "Is that . . . an F-16XL?"

It was a very rare plane—and it *was* his. At least at some point in his past it had been. Or at some point in another time and place.

But here it was, again.

That persistent vision of something speeding by him in a blur?

It had been this. This incredible flying machine.

His airplane.

Another missing part, found.

"We don't know where or how the AII guys got it," St. Louis explained. "But those things in the other displays came from 'somewhere else.' So we have to assume this came from somewhere else, too."

One side of the glass case had been taken down. Hunter walked up to the planeand gently touched it.

That's when the lightning bolt hit again.

Suddenly he started remembering the strangest things: falling into the ocean "somewhere else" and encountering immense naval ships. Taking part in a titanic war, much like World War II, but entirely different. Trying to save America by fighting battles far from home. He'd even had a different name; he'd been called "Sky Ghost."

Then suddenly he was in outer space, fighting against a huge galactic empire. He closed his eyes and saw constellations. Star clusters. They all looked so familiar, as if he'd flown between them, going faster than anyone could imagine. And he felt there were people out there whom he loved and respected, whom he'd fought with. But who were they? And, more important, *where* were they?

He didn't know. And as soon as he took his hand off the airplane, the sensation quickly faded away.

He felt better, though, because half of the emptiness inside him had been filled.

But what about the other half?

The mysterious blonde, the angel who was always waving to him?

Who was she?

Again, St. Louis read his mind.

"They asked us not force memories on you," he told Hunter. "But if you remember this airplane, then you should also remember . . . her."

"You know about her?" Hunter asked.

St. Louis nodded. Everyone who knew Hawk Hunter knew his longtime girlfriend. She was beautiful beyond words, a girl he'd met on the battlefield of Europe after World War III whom he'd loved throughout all the calamities that followed.

St. Louis said, "That flag you had with you when you arrived. Do you still have it?"

Hunter had carried it with him everywhere since getting it back. He took it out of his breast pocket.

"Did you ever unfold it?" St. Louis asked.

Hunter shook his head no.

"I didn't dare to," he said. "I didn't want it to fall apart."

St. Louis smiled. "Don't worry—that flag will *never* fall apart."

Hunter turned it over in his hands. It almost seemed too fragile to unravel.

"It's okay," St. Louis urged him. "Unfold it . . . "

Hunter did—and inside he found an old, weathered picture of the mysterious blonde.

He was instantly transfixed.

And finally he knew who she was.

Dominique . . .

His long-lost love.

"You see, Hawk?" St. Louis told him. "We had to come all the way out here to find your airplane. But her? She's been with you all along."

Hunter couldn't speak for a long time. Then he turned to St. Louis.

"All my answers," he said, almost choking up. "Finally . . . "

Dr. Pott walked over to them.

"Everything in here is an example of things just slightly out of time," Pott said to Hunter. "And that's what I think you are too, my friend. The difference is, now you understand it."

Hunter looked at the picture again. His heart was breaking.

He said, "I know who she is. But . . . I think she might be . . . dead."

Pott looked at Dominique's picture.

"She might have passed on in some other universe," he said. "But there's a very good chance she's still with us in this one. Remember: infinite possibilities. I'm no shrink, but I suggest you go look for her as soon as possible."

St. Louis nodded. "I agree—but right now, let's get the hell out of here."

It took only fifteen minutes to move Hunter's F-16XL out onto the runway.

He checked out its systems himself—and to his astonishment everything was working perfectly, as though he'd just climbed out of it minutes before. He lit its powerful engines, and they were soon humming flawlessly.

He couldn't remember feeling such joy.

He and his kick-ass F-16XL—together again.

"It's good to be back," he said aloud.

By this time, all of the homeless people had been loaded onto the C-119s and the Boxcars were airborne. The B-25s went next.

Then Hunter took off in the XL, saluting the old, battered, and now-burning base as he rose into the sky. Ben was flying the indefatigable F-86 beside him. Way off in the distance, they could see the trio of huge AMC cargo planes slowly approaching in the early morning light. But the Football City raiding party would be long gone before the AMC paratroopers arrived. The mission was over, as was the bloodshed.

The strange collection of airplanes formed up and, as one, turned east.

It was time to go home.

Dr. Pott and St. Louis wound up back on the B-25 that JT was driving.

It was in the lead of the prop-driven planes. Hunter's XL was off to its left, going slow and protecting the air convoy from any potential threats. Ben was doing the same thing in the Sabre, flying off to their right.

Pott had had a very unusual experience on the ground at Groom Lake. Even while battles raged above and below ground, he'd spent the time reading through the recovered AII data. He'd come upon some incredible findings.

Once they were safely away from the Groom Lake area, he started going through some of the written files taken from the AII storage room and stayed at it over the next few hours.

Finally he made his way up to the B-25's flight deck and, in bits and pieces, related what he'd found to JT and St. Louis.

First of all, he confirmed that the AII team members had indeed been jumping universes.

But how?

"Believe it or not, they were doing it by getting 'shot' by the big ray gun," Pott revealed to them. "I don't know where they got it or how it was built, but that apparatus was not designed to kill people like the AMC thought, but to send them 'somewhere else.' "

St. Louis couldn't believe it. "So you mean in some other universe, there's a bunch of homeless people and a bunch of old army trucks?"

Pott nodded. "That's seems to be the case."

St. Louis groaned. "Damn—and we just made a grilled cheese out of that thing."

JT piped up, "Does it say in there anywhere why we would see that guy in black jump into the bottomless pit with a parachute? Who was he? And where does that hole go anyhow? We saw them blowing embers down there. Maybe they weren't embers at all."

Pott just shook his head. "I haven't found anything on that yet," he said. "I'll keep looking. But, hold on tight, because I've got more bombshells to lay on you . . . "

Pott said he'd found some of the last reports written by the AII team before the project folded. As it turned out, they'd stayed out at Groom Lake for at least several years after the Big War, continuing their research until they themselves suddenly vanished.

"It also turns out they had a lot of data on our friend, Major Hunter," Pott told them, looking through one of the last boxes he'd recovered. "They followed his exploits through a number of different universes even though Hunter himself isn't aware of these adventures, as evidenced by his confusion and memory loss when he arrived here.

"But the strange thing is, no matter where he wound up, he was always on hand to help save the day for the forces of good against the forces of evil."

"Why does that not surprise me?" JT asked.

Pott went on, "But here's the scary part: while we know there might be an infinite number of you and me and everyone on this plane in an infinite number of universes, the AII team came to believe there was only one Hawk Hunter and that he was continually bouncing back and forth between universes, always showing up in times of need and saving the day.

"In other words, there's *not* an infinite number of Hawk Hunters. There's only one, in an infinite number of universes."

St. Louis and JT just shook their heads upon hearing this. It seemed very way-out, yet Pott seemed deadly serious.

He continued, "My AII colleagues looked into this further and discovered that the odds of having just one person falling from universe to universe by chance and always saving the day were astronomically incalculable, or better put, literally 'inconceivable.' "

At that point, he stopped to reread a note that had been included at the bottom of the last AII report he could find on Hunter's exploits. It said his colleagues had concluded that in the scope of all human science and history, only two words could describe why Hunter was doing what he was doing.

But their conclusion was so mind-blowing, Pott couldn't even read it aloud. So he handed the report to St. Louis instead.

Hastily scrawled at the bottom, it read: "Only conclusion possible: Divine Intervention."

At that moment, they finally saw Football City on the horizon.

They were back home.

They saw the F-16XL pull out in front of them and do a series of eye-popping spins. Then Hunter boosted the plane's power plants to full throttle and was off, heading east at full afterburner.

"He's going to look for her," JT said simply. "I hope he finds her."

As the F-16XL climbed into the sky, St. Louis, still awed by what he'd just read, managed to say, "I just hope he doesn't wait another ten years before he comes back again."

ABOUT THE AUTHOR

Mack Maloney is the author of numerous fiction series, including Wingman, Chopper Ops, Starhawk, and Pirate Hunters, as well as *UFOs in Wartime: What They Didn't Want You to Know*. A native Bostonian, Maloney received a bachelor of science degree in journalism at Suffolk University and a master of arts degree in film at Emerson College. He is the host of a national radio show, *Mack Maloney's Military X-Files*.

WINGMAN EBOOKS

FROM OPEN ROAD MEDIA

Available wherever ebooks are sold

OPEN ROAD
INTEGRATED MEDIA

Open Road Integrated Media is a digital publisher and multimedia content company. Open Road creates connections between authors and their audiences by marketing its ebooks through a new proprietary online platform, which uses premium video content and social media.

Videos, Archival Documents, and New Releases

Sign up for the Open Road Media newsletter and get news delivered straight to your inbox.

Sign up now at
www.openroadmedia.com/newsletters

Lightning Source UK Ltd.
Milton Keynes UK
UKOW04f0645210415

250012UK00001B/34/P